RETURN TO WILLIAM'S POINT

A LEGENDS OF WILLIAM'S POINT SHORT STORY ANTHOLOGY VOLUME 2

M.D. MARTIN

DEDICATION

This book is dedicated to the memory of my father, Rickie Martin, you always challenged me to push myself and not take shortcuts when it came to creativity. I thank you for the lessons starting in childhood when I brought you a picture I had drawn and you told me to go back and do it again without tracing it. At the time I thought that was harsh but as I have looked back on it throughout the years I know it was meant to make me push myself to create my own masterpieces, not regurgitate someone else's work. It has made me a stronger artist whether in the world of art or in the world of literary works. Thank you.

CONTENTS

1   The Hybrid's Daughter   1

2   Micah   24

3   The Mansion   36

4   The Witches   43

5   Interlude 1 – Seth's Birth   48

6   No Trespassing   52

7   Interlude 2 – Seth's Mother   58

8   Albatross   61

9   Resurrection   71

INTRODUCTION

The limbs of the trees clattered together like hollow bones in the dry autumn breeze. The whickering call of a night bird joined the ghostly melody as the ethereal scent of wood smoke whispered on the wind. Autumn had returned to William's Point. It had crept in on silent feet and had begun to nestle down amongst the Blue Ridge mountains.

A dense fog drifted lazily amongst the night blackened tree trunks and draped the primordial forest in its tattered spectral shroud. What strange creatures lurked in its deathly embrace? What frightening monsters of old once again roamed the land? What fiends of Hell had clawed their way towards Heaven only to be vomited up by the Earth that had once lovingly embraced them? What new freedom, strange and intoxicating, did they feel as once again they roamed the land and saw with eyes no longer dimmed by cob webs or crusted with the dusts of centuries. They were alive once more......

THE HYBRID'S DAUGHTER

I have tasted blood. I have felt its intoxicating slide as it feeds my veins with its ruby nectar of life. I have experienced the bitter after taste of death as it settles on my taste buds and drifts into my unconscious dreams. I have witnessed the milky film that covers the eyes of my victims and for one brief moment I weep for them.

I am the last of my breed. I am the only one that has survived from the ill-timed accident of my father. He was a hybrid and although he does not know of my existence I know of his. I know of his every move and thought and I know that even now he waits for me although he is unaware of it. He has called to me from the wilderness of our ravaged souls and I am answering him.

I must feed from the flesh of the human; I cannot tolerate the flesh of an animal. My senses are more powerful than my fathers. I am the genetic cross breed of the hybrid; I am what the government has made me. They took the blood from my father and tested it, purified it and made me; the warrior they wanted to control for battle; the devourer that would not die but gain strength from the death of my enemies.

I was fed for eighteen long years and kept in a lab full of stainless steel and glass cubicles. My body was pushed to its limits and still I gained strength. The more they drained me, the more power I possessed. I smile now as I think back on my father's torment. How they locked him in a hospital for years and took his blood. They observed him night and day and went to the near edge of obsession with his abilities.

Now on this night of nights, I go to him, to save him from his enemies and to save myself. I waited until the nurses' gave me the fateful pills that always rob me of my identity; the drugs they use to control my mind, to slow my body, to make me sleep an unnatural sleep devoid of dreams. I waited until the lights were out and then I crept from my bed to the window.

The thin mesh of wires that covered the window was nothing compared to the need within me for freedom. I felt little pain as the glass dug into my hands while I pushed with all my strength against it. I felt the glass give and then burst under the strain. Blood streamed from the many cuts on my hands as I silently licked it from my fingers. Tonight I would go out into the world that was hiding my father and then we would go to William's Point and find the sisters that had made us.

Two a.m. and the streets were deserted as I walked down the narrow alleys, trying to avoid the silent beams of the spotlights on the police cars. I wrapped my arms around my waist as I attempted to fend off the cold moist air. My long black hair streamed into my face as I felt the crunch of broken glass beneath my bare feet. I felt no real pain, not pain as defined by humans; I felt only mild irritation at the disturbance.

My sense of direction was keen and soon I was standing in front of a small run down house on the seedier side of town. I was able to acquire the needed clothing from the small supply in the back as the couple lay sleeping in the next room. I never made a sound as I dressed in a pair of ragged old blue jeans and a cut off tee shirt that left my taunt stomach exposed and clung to my full breasts. I looked like the proverbial teenage rebel that I had heard the nurses talk about during their breaks. They had discussed their children, daughters in particular, and how they never seemed to listen to common sense.

I stared for a moment at myself in the age speckled mirror that hung over the sink in their bathroom, seeing myself for the first time in my eighteen years. My hair hung well past my waist and was the color of jet, my eyes were dark bottomless pools of black and I had inherited my mother's Native American features. My cheekbones were high and proud and my nose was aquiline, taken from my father's fine boned stock. My full lips parted slightly as I surveyed my sharp k-9s and I grinned almost impishly as I was reminded of the awed gasps of the doctors when they had first viewed my teeth.

I left the bathroom but paused to stand in the cramped little bedroom, staring silently at the couple laying in blissful slumber beneath the tattered covers. They were dreaming of winning the lottery and what they would do with the money. The woman dreamt of saving their daughter from her life on the streets. The husband dreamt of taking his sister-in-law to Bermuda. The images that followed were foreign to me, I knew nothing of the relationships between a man and a woman and the brief flashes of naked bodies writhing together on the sand made little sense to me. I knew only of the ecstasy I felt when I fed. I shrugged as the lewd images played through my head like some disjointed movie frames then turned to leave. I spied the beat-up pair of Nike's tucked haphazardly under the edge of the broken down Barco lounger and stopped to slip them on enjoying the fit of the worn shoes and testing their flexibility. They would do. I left the couple alive and dreaming of their secret fantasies, I don't know why but I couldn't bring myself to kill them it was one of my rare moments of consciousness.

I traveled that first night, through the dirt smudged streets toward the horizon and my father. I slept in the bus stations and fed off the bastards that wanted to do the same thing with me that I had seen in the poor man's dreams. I was repulsed by their overtures and felt dirty after they had tried to touch me; my only pleasure was when I stalked them afterwards and fed off of their filthy blood. I learned much in that first week of freedom. The hospital had been a blessing in disguise.

I made friends with the hookers who sold their bodies for the burden of man; money. Many of them needed it to eat, some to support the habit of the smoky drugs that sang through their veins and others for the simple pleasure of desecrating themselves with the vile stench of a stranger. Whatever their reasons, they were out there every night pushing themselves at the passing cars not scared of what may be waiting for them.

I felt sorry for them. An emotion I wasn't used to feeling. My program is supposed to be devoid of emotions and yet I was feeling things for these people. The one time I did feed from one of them I was ill for two weeks afterward. I remember it distinctly. Sister Maria, as everyone on the streets called her, was a tragic woman who had lost all hope of a future other than the one she had chosen. My heart had gone out to her and I felt for the first time the torment of a soul whose wings had been broken.

I found her one night after she had been with one of her many customers. She had been beaten for the millionth time since I had met her and I held her while she silently wept the dry tears of someone who had gotten used to their lot in life. I rocked her gently and marveled at the maternal feelings that swam through my blood. I never knew my mother she had long since left the hospital before I was old enough to remember her. I only knew what I had found in the medical records and in the minds of the doctors and nurses. She had been pretty through, seductive in her dark features and bountiful body.

Maria had been bound for the sisterhood before she had taken a drastic turn for the worse. She had fallen in with a married man and had been publicly humiliated by him when she thought there was more to their relationship than sex. From that point on she hadn't cared about anything, she had taken refuge on the street instead of going to the Order and begging for forgiveness. She had felt that her penance should be played and spread eagle beneath the scum of the earth, to use her milky white body and alabaster skin for their torment. A torment that twisted in her soul with its steely coils and slowly wrung the life from her until there was nothing left of the old Maria.

She had taken me in and given me a place to live while she worked her way through life, passing all the things that held beauty to most people with a blind eye. She no longer enjoyed anything about being alive and I had watched as she declined beyond alcohol and drug addiction into a realm devoid of life, devoid of pleasure, a realm of self-imposed exile. She shielded herself from the slings and arrows of the world by turning a cold shoulder to everyone, everyone except me. For some odd reason she had let me in and even confided in me about her past. That's what urged me to give her the way out that she had been looking for all these years.

Her tormented face stared blankly up at me with its broken blue eyes that implored me for some sort of salvation. I knew I couldn't deny her the one final present, the kiss of death that I carried as my birthright.

"I can make it all go away forever," I whispered as I held her close and felt the pain that went beyond physical.

"Forever," she echoed as she turned her neck up in a silent plea for me to stop the madness that had gripped her for so long.

I was tender with this broken dove that lay in my arms and after I had drained the blood from her I wept. I held her cold body and cried the tears she hadn't been able to cry in all those long years. She had been dead before I took her blood and now I had set her free. I carried her body out of the oil slickened city, into the surrounding country where she could really be free and buried her deep in the rich dark soil.

"Rest peacefully," I mumbled as I turned back to the lights of the city.

A slight rain began and it was through this mist that I walked as if drugged by something foreign. I had never felt the nausea that was now welling up in my body and soon I was bent over double with spasms in my stomach. I emptied the churning contents on the quickly damping ground and curled up into a fetal position. Misery that was the only term besides pure hell that I could use to describe what I was feeling.

The rain picked up and I was soon soaked clean through but I was somewhere far off from my physical self. I was soaring through the clouds into the starry night above the storm, riding the winds that pushed the rain on. My mind was unable to focus and my body shook as if in the grips of some violent fever. I could feel my spirit animal as it approached me and when I opened my eyes I found a solid white wolf standing there above me. Its pale golden eyes stared deeply into my own and I felt its mind reaching out to me. It was a reassurance that I needed as I lay there sure that the spirit horse was coming for me.

He lay down beside me and curled his large body around mine, giving me his warm fur to bury my face in. I held tight to the wild animal, never questioning his decision to stay by me. I don't know how long I lay there in that position walking through that burning hell that Maria's blood had induced in my body. I imagined myself moving beside the wolf, wandering through the green leafed trees along a lane. I could hear the roaring waves of the ocean as they crashed against the sandy shore and I felt the warmth of my father just beyond the rock outcropping.

In my mind I approached the house and walked up the wooden steps, the wolf following close by my side. I could feel him in the bedroom at the top of the stairs and I could feel something more, something black and filled with hate and menace. I could feel the pain that was ripping into his soul with its tiny terrible claws. I pushed the door open and found his towering frame gazing down upon a small figure curled in the silk sheets in the middle of the bed. She was dark and beautiful but I could see beyond her closed eyelids and I saw the truth. The ugly truth that stared back at me with her taunting eyes and viciously grinning mouth. She was too full of hate to love anyone besides herself and I knew that this was one of his enemies who wooed him with loving words filled with deception and venomous promises of a different tomorrow.

So this was the tormentor, the one who enslaved my father and made him pray for mercy, this was the one I had to defeat to free him. Cold blackness, that's what I felt for her and I knew that I would eventually have to kill her. I thought of actually taking her life, of feeding slowly while she screamed for him to help her. I would enjoy it. My attention was drawn back to the tragic beauty of my father as one thought ran through his mind, *May God have mercy on my soul.* I had dreamt of this before, I recognized the line from my nightmares. He begged for forgiveness from God and asked for deliverance from his hell. It was the call that had brought me from my drug induced slumber some weeks ago.

"Father!" I cried out and tried to throw my arms around him, to comfort him.

He turned quickly and I knew he had heard me but stared at me as if he couldn't comprehend my sudden appearance. Or maybe he couldn't see me at all. I was unsure but I knew that this was the reason I had broken out of the hospital and I now had to get back to my body to free myself of the burning hell that was writhing like a serpent in my insides. Shock registered on his beautiful face as he reached out to grab me.

I awoke from the dream and lay listening to the soft breathing of the wolf as it rested beside me, sharing its warmth. A tear slipped down my cheek as I felt the cold rain washing over my body and the desolation of being without my family. I, too, felt like begging forgiveness from the divine entity that my father was crying out to.

Another image came to me, an image of gossamer gowns and alabaster skin. Bare shoulders now unmarred by the ugly bruises that had only hours ago darkened the pale shimmering skin. Her hair fell in a halo of blonde locks about her and her serene face registered kindness not the harsh lines that had been permanently etching into it. Her touch was cool against my burning skin bringing strength to my limbs and helping me to rise from the soggy ground. Not a word did she speak but held my arm firmly and walked with me as if we were merely strolling down a boulevard. My wolf followed closely as if this were an everyday occurrence. Light shone around us as she led me past the trees that had blocked my view of the city, farther out back towards the smoke choked metropolis with its sin infested streets.

"Tonight you came to me in my time of need, now I repay the favor," she whispered as she led me down a twisting path toward some unknown tree lined lane in the better part of town.

I saw lights through a blurred kaleidoscope of colors and the cacophony of noises that assaulted my ears were like the lilting sounds of angel's voices on high. I tried to keep my bearings straight but we moved through the streets like a wraith and I knew that I would never find my way back across this path.

We finally came to a stop at the doorway of an expensive two story brownstone townhouse. When I turned to ask who lived here, she was gone and I was left alone except for my wolf. The strength left my limbs and I felt the earth tilt and whirl beyond my control. Just as I began to fall I was caught in a strong embrace and the soft comforting words were whispered in my ear.

"Shhh, it's alright little one. I'm here now," his soothing voice reached my muddled mind through its fog and wrapped me in a blanket of protection.

I woke again, staring up at the skylights that bathed me in a soft moonlight. My body was no longer in the fetal position I had fallen back in to after Maria had left me but I was still sick, still ill from the blood she had given me.

"Rest little one, don't try to think about the future," again the soothing voice encircled me with its protectiveness.

"I must leave," I tried to sit up but fell back again.

"Rest," the tone hardened with warning, "you're safe now."

I lay there listening to the rain pelting against the domed glass overhead and wished he would talk some more. Who was he? Where had he come from? What would he do to me? Why was I feeling this way? What was happening to me?

"I told you not to think about the future. You're as stubborn as your father," he mumbled as he approached the bed and came in to the moonlight.

My breath caught in my throat as I stared up in to eyes as dark as mine and the same Native American features.

"Shh, calm down I'm no apparition. My name used to be Abraham; I no longer go by that though. My name is Gypsy and you have no name my dear sweet little one. They never gave you a name only a number. I will have to fix that won't I? Now before you crease that beautiful brow again I suppose I should tell you who I am. I am the one that created your father. I am your grandfather," his statement astonished me.

I stared harder at his youthful features and knew that I was looking at a relative but surely not my grandfather.

"How?" I asked as he sat down beside me on the bed and ran a hand across my fevered brow.

"When we reach a certain age our true nature overrides this mortal coil we were born into. I have been the same age for eighty-two years but I have matured in wisdom and knowledge. You will continue to grow, to evolve so long as I can keep you alive long enough my sweetling. Drink this, it will help with the fever," his kindness cascaded over me as he lifted my head to sip from a pewter vessel pressed to my lips.

The rich thick blood filled my mouth and cleansed my palette then raced down my burning throat to splash in my clenched belly. A moan tore from my throat and I knew the blood was going to come rushing back up in a matter of minutes.

"Shh, it will be alright. I must replace the poisoned blood you lost with my own clean blood. Your friend poisoned you with her alcohol and drugs, poor thing; you're ignorant in so many ways. It's my fault for letting your father go for so long in that damnable place before I called him out into the world. I was foolish then and didn't want to admit my mistakes. I need to make amends now, so I will start with you. We don't need to go to William's Point; there is nothing there but heartache. We will get you well first and then we will go and collect your father. Then we will start our lives out as a family, are you listening to me?"

I had stopped listening when he told me that we would not be going to William's Point.

"I must go to William's Point, I don't know why but I have to go," I tried again to get up but it was no use.

He smiled a warm entreaty meant to comfort me but I knew that he was only humoring me. Well let him think what he would, I knew that as soon as I got well I would leave. I would go and rescue my father and then we would travel to William's Point and that would be that.

"Willful child," he admonished and forced me to drink again.

The rest of the night passed in amiable silence as he alternately forced me to drink and then held me as my body convulsed and I emptied the contents of my stomach over and over again. I swore that he was adding to my hell with the pungent blood he was making me drink. He only laughed and continued to administer his hateful helpfulness. I say hateful because in my state of mind it was hateful, I see now that he was only saving me from the venomous demon I had ingested from Maria, rest her soul.

For two weeks I fought the demons of hell as they tried to consume me within their gapping maws. For two weeks the man that now called himself Gypsy helped and comforted me, staying by my bedside until the last of the devil's own hell fires left my body. I was gaunt and lifeless on the last day of my fever and he knew that I needed nourishment.

"Tonight you will come with me to hunt, you will take over your body once more and make it obey your commands," he whispered beside my ear when I refused to look upon his handsome face again.

I stared blankly through the long silky tresses of black hair that draped across my face at a spot on the wall. I had stared at that spot a million times in the last couple of weeks and wondered where Maria had ascended to after she left me. I had stepped inside the circle of her private hell and survived it. Why couldn't she have made it out alive? Why had she courted death? Why had I given in and given her the only thing she wanted? Neitzche once said, "That which does not kill me makes me stronger." I am proof of that and after I fed that night, there was no stopping me.

I became sister to the fates while I stood at the threshold of hell and held the demons hands as they ate at my flesh. I was pushed farther than the doctors had ever dreamed and I was stronger than Gypsy had surmised. I had become what neither he nor my father ever could, I was a killer born and bred but the only thing I could not kill was a child.

I left that night, after I had fed and have not seen Gypsy until recently. We all met again in William's Point but I shall continue with my story before I lead you astray. I had fed all night with Gypsy and he begged me not to leave him but I could not stay.

"There are so many things I need to tell you," he whispered as he caressed my hair in the early morning glow of sunrise.

"I can't stay," I replied as I watched the sun burnish the sky with pinks and golds.

"I know. Maybe we'll meet again in William's Point and maybe then you'll be ready listen to everything I have to say," again he caressed my hair and then he kissed me on the cheek.

A small sad smile curled my lips as I vaulted over the railing and disappeared into the trees.

I traveled by night mostly, not because of any great necessity but simply because I preferred the solace of the moon as she guided my feet. My wolf came to me many times and walked along with me, helping me to find my way through the darkened tree lined back roads. We were as one and his thoughts were my thoughts, together we spoke in the silent language of the elders, the ones that had come before the white man. The elders that used to carry on the stories of the great ones and pass on the knowledge of life, the mysteries of the medicines and darkness of the spirits that walked through the night on silent feet and dwelled in the borderlands between here and what lies beyond. We were one and the same and I felt his power singing through my veins when I grew tired or hungry.

I fed very little during my journey from the boiling hot western coast to the cooler climate of the east. I saw many things in the dead of night that would curdle the blood of men but I passed these things by without a backward glance, moving like a slender wisp of smoke between the hulking trunks of moon silvered trees. I stayed away from humanity in their crowded city walls and rat infested tenants. I enjoyed the fresh air and the smell of the outdoors. My hunger was appeased every so often when I found a lost soul fearing the darkness and trying to find some sort of shelter. I felt no pity, no remorse, I simply felt the ecstasy of the blood and I loved it.

My mind was focused on one thing and one thing only. My father was somewhere on the seaboard and I was going to find him. Eve. She loomed up in front of me every time I tried to picture him in my head. Her ugly grinning countenance as she warned me away. He belonged to her and she wouldn't give him up without a fight. Well, that would make it sweeter wouldn't it?

Hate, I felt it again and I became a good friend to it. It writhed in my body and soul and I nourished it with contempt, fed it with distrust and sullenness. I welcomed its cold embrace and longed for its biting sarcasm. I would enjoy killing her, was looking forward to it, and I would make sure she felt every agonizing second of it. It had become a quest to disembowel this woman, to let her lie screaming in agony in a pool of her own blood and I was reminded of the footage of wars the doctors had made me watch constantly.

They had taunted me with the scent of blood and the videos of carnage and they had been sexually aroused by my reactions. The blood lust that had filmed my eyes and sharpened the colors, the rosy glow of my skin and the wildness that had taken hold of me. I hadn't been the fool they did far too well in that area for me to usurp their position. I had been too careful to mask my true reactions to the bloody combat, the excitement I too was feeling.

The days passed in blurred succession and I was happy to finally find myself wondering into the small town with cobblestone streets and crashing ocean waves. The boardwalk that stretched in an endless bleached bone mass along the powdered sand and the lively music that echoed from a club down the street at the corner. The club my father had frequented before her and the hell she loved to subject him to. I went to the condo that he had lived in for a brief time and met the two men that knew Randolph intimately.

Jarred and Michael were humorous in their constant arguments about Randolph and they seemed to know me just by my features. Of course they assumed I was

Storm's sister, they would never have believed that I was his daughter and I wasn't about to try to explain it to them. Instead they welcomed me into the warmth of the jet set laid back lifestyle and helped me to become accustomed to social graces. I care little for what fork to use or how to flirt with visiting dignitaries but they felt that before I could circulate in my *brother's* world, I needed to be refined.

I only allowed them this little pleasure because Storm was out of the country with his heathen of a wife and I had time to waste while I waited for him to return. Time to plan my next move and how to dispose of her body afterward. Time, it is a distortion by which mortals gauge their lives; what a pity. I have little use for the idea of time only for its basis of light and darkness. What good is time to someone who cannot age, who doesn't live by a clock on the wall?

Alas, Jarred and Michael were able to take the unrefined and create something out of it. I was dressed properly even though I still preferred little to nothing as far as clothing went. I was presented to society and passed with flying colors even though it behooved me to put on airs for the hypocrites that flaunted their wealth and supposed humanitarian efforts for the homeless. Never once had one of them offered to help anyone even close to the likes of Maria or myself. Scum, we had been street scum that they scrapped from the soles of their shoes before they entered Tiffany's for breakfast or the Porsche dealership to trade in last year's model for a new one. Recycled garbage spit up by the cracks in the sidewalk and they had never hesitated to make us feel that way. Only good for one thing and that was what Maria had made her profession.

She would have thought it grand that I was now moving among them in their tight little circles and being considered a lady of potential, a lady of means and importance. I often smiled to myself as some distinguished gentleman whispered in my ear of his latest trip to the Alps and thought of how Maria would be enjoying every second of the masquerade.

It was during one of these dinner parties that I met him. He was a tall man in his mid-twenties with long flowing hair and flashing eyes the color of star spangled midnight sky. He was a solitary figure that often stood back and watched the crowd. Sometimes he would indulge in conversation with one of the laughing females or the more solemn men that liked to hover around the hearths and try to covet the *serious* political conversations.

Like I said before, time is what mortals guide their lives by and in all the centuries of this world their social habits have hardly changed. Every once in a while a brave feminine soul would try to break into this inner circle that was dominated by testosterone but they didn't last long, either they walked away in a huff because their sensibilities had been affronted or they practically broke out in a brawl when they didn't see eye to eye. I found it amusing, I could have easily stepped in and conversed with the best of them on the state of affairs today but why should I? Why should I care what men discussed among their own kind, I wasn't there for them or the tall stranger who leered at me when I wasn't looking.

Instead I became engrossed by the less blustery voices of the intellectuals, the ones that always try to hide their natures from the rest because they would be eaten by the sharks if their true identities were known. I have found that in society there are still class distinctions, upper of the upper, politically correct, and those of us who conceal our true nature, the outcasts if you will. There are outcasts at every party and sooner or later we always gravitate toward each other. It became a habit to seek them out before the party actually got started just for the sheer comfort of knowing I wouldn't be alone the rest of evening.

I'm not saying that I wasn't lured into many of the other conversations that swam about me; as a matter of fact it became a game to the political bullies to try to connect with me in some way. Most times they simply wanted to connect with me in the basest of ways, much like the dreams of the poor man a lifetime ago. I didn't mind, I grinned my way graciously through the dribble like Jarred and Michael had taught me to but I knew deep down that I hated being refined. I hated being a lady and most of all I hated these people that called themselves my new friends. No wonder my father was slowly going insane, I would too if I had to endure this for any length of time.

It was during one of the first summer parties that I was approached by my brooding stranger. It was a yacht party and my hostess was Mrs. Jeanette Dupree, a middle aged widow from the south of France. She was sweet in her own way but her husband's death had sent her swinging the other way. I tried to stay away from her as best as possible without being rude, I didn't return the feelings. It was ironic to me that I was experiencing the same thing my father had with Jarred and Michael, what a parallel life we were living.

I had taken solitude on the uppermost deck of the yacht, enjoying the salty sea spray and the fresh air. I had grown tired of the usual conversations that swirled amidst the stale cigar smoke and the pungent aroma of champagne as it sparkled in diamond cut crystal flutes. I had also grown tired of the lascivious looks I was attracting not only from the political bullies but from my hostess as well and I only hoped that she hadn't followed me above deck. Of course I would be able to handle the matter more delicately if she had. Instead the almost silent treat that caught my keen ears was that of my dark stranger.

He was farther down the deck, just coming up the stairs when I heard his soft breathing and the soft tread of his footsteps. He had obviously grown tired of the same old thing as well. If only my father would return soon, I could leave this forsaken place filled with pleasant vipers and get back out into the real world instead of this disjointed fairy tale from hell. I tried to pay attention to his strikingly handsome figure as he strolled along the pristine white deck in his black tie and tux.

I so hate formal attire, it's a bother to dress up to show off. I smiled as I thought of the females pouting prettily downstairs and wondering where this smooth tongued devil had disappeared to. He really did have a power over them, but that was nothing compared to the power my father possessed. Oh well, maybe I should jump ship and swim back to shore. A fine sight that would be, with my blood red evening gown trailing through the water, surely I would attract the wolves of the sea with their rows of sharpened teeth. A slight laugh bubbled out of my throat as I imagined the sharks circling just below the surface, their lifeless eyes glaring up through the gloom at my gown as it taunted them now.

"What an imagination you have," the soft lulling words were like a whisper of wind without substance.

Had I imagined them?

"Of course you didn't, you're cleverer than that," again the words swept more over my mind than my body.

I turned to look at the lower end of the deck and ran directly into his chest. A smooth wall of hardened flesh hiding beneath the silk of his shirt. It rippled as my nose buried itself in the soft material and I was assaulted with the smell of some unknown but dusky cologne surely made to drive women crazy. Steely arms wrapped around me as I was forced to stand closer to this mountain of slow sexual tension lurking behind the guise of a man.

"My but you're a sensual beast, and here you had me believing you wanted nothing to do with sex or the thought of it," he was so smug and I was furious with my mind and his ability to read it.

"I am not," I replied indignantly only realizing after it came out how childish it sounded.

A low chuckle started somewhere in his chest and radiated out to wash over me in sparkling waves.

"Let me go," I demanded shoving against that rock chest.

"What are you going to do, call for daddy?" taunts from this man were like needles under my skin.

"Let me go," I warned once more, my voice changing, lowering to a menacing growl.

"No need for that. I thought you would be fun, but I suppose not, I should have listened to Micah and never come near you. Ah, what sweet folly, now not only do I have you to contend with but Micah as well," he sighed deeply and stepped back.

Now that I was free, I pressed myself as close to the railing as I could. I glared up at his moon washed face and tried to fathom his mind, it was a wall of silence that he would not allow me to penetrate.

"Who's Micah?" I asked, leaving off at my attempt to read him.

"You'll see. I must warn you though, you don't want to meet him or else you will surely die. I was supposed to give you this message, don't go to William's Point, it can only bring you heartache. There's nothing there for you, I promise you that, nothing you need to know about," he turned from me and stared out at the ocean.

"Who are you?" I moved to stand beside him sensing his thoughts more than hearing them.

"Who I am is not important, you are lucky that Micah bid me not to taste of you. You are an abomination to us, our natural enemy. Your father, your grandfather, your clan must never mix with ours for surely there will be nothing but death as an outcome," his voice trailed off to mix with the waves that lapped against the hull.

"What are you?" I placed my hand on his shoulder and felt the chill that slipped out from beneath his overcoat.

"Touch me and you die," it wasn't a threat but it prompted me to be perverse.

"Then I do touch, and now do I die?" I asked as I raised a brow and held my breath as he tensed.

"You are truly and enemy to be wary of. Micah will enjoy this hunting trip," his voice was an echo of faraway.

"I think you're scared. Do I frighten you?" I couldn't help this sudden urge to push him.

He turned suddenly and I was amazed at his reddened eyes and the beautiful perfect fangs that peeked from beneath his upper lip. A half grin pulled at my mouth and I knew a perverse ecstasy and a sudden need to laugh. I fought the urge but it was still there, maybe it was hysteria I don't know.

"Heed my words or die. Do not go to William's Point. Do not try to seek out the witches or find anything of a past worth forgetting. You will only come to an end that you would rather not meet just yet. I promise you that if your clan comes within the limits of William's Point you will be killed. If I could find you this easily what makes you think we can't find you again. For your own sake, put off this battle until the time of the prophecy, do not provoke Micah, you'll only end up dead and for some reason he won't impart to me, he's reluctant to kill you.

Better for you and your clan to stay away then put temptation to the test. This is your only warning," he growled as he backed away from me and then disappeared down the stairwell to the deck below.

I stood there with the stars shining overhead and was filled with a savage pride to pick up the challenge just thrown at my feet. Death would be their best bet if they thought I would cave in to their whims. I would go to William's Point now or know the reason why, no one was going to tell me where I could go and where I couldn't. My clan would return to their birthplace and I would find the witches and eat their black hearts if I so desired and no dark avenging demon with fanged teeth was going to stop me. Vampire or no, I was going to William's Point.

It wasn't long after that night that I became aware of more than one set of eyes watching me. They were everywhere, you just had to know how to spot them but I was amazed at how I had missed this before. I had had my mind so set on William's Point and getting there that I had completely ignored the silent rogues that seemed to follow me everywhere. At night I would hear them whispering in the alleyways as I visited the small club on the corner and see them on the dance floor as they grinned at the humans then lured them to their death. At least I didn't make any false promises, I thought as I walked silently back to the condo, uncaring of their thinly veiled threat.

I suppose I flaunted myself in their faces, not scared of their urgent need to take me. They all wanted to break my neck, to taste my blood but they were afraid to, either because of some superstition or this one called Micah. Whatever the reason for their fear I played upon it, I fed that need to a fever pitch and yet, I continued to even when they began to become braver.

Once I awoke with one staring down at me as I lay in bed, watching me sleep. I didn't hesitate only reacted like a coil that had been wound too tight. I leapt from the bed and wrestled him to the floor. Strength was matched with strength and I found that I was caught in a steely grip as his fangs pressed against my throat. As he broke the skin and my blood began to flow I heard the growl from somewhere beyond the small puddle of moonlight, somewhere in the dark confines of my bedroom.

The glow of yellow eyes winked from the darkness and then the howl of pain as the great furry blur passed over my shoulder and landed head on into the creature that had held me. I turned in time to see the wolf sinking its own fangs into the soft neck and ripping the muscle and sinew from the throat. His paws dug feverishly as he continued to rip the throat open and great bursts of blood flowed from the wounds. The vampire fought frantically, pulling at the thick coat of the wolf and howling in pain as it finally got free. I stared, transfixed as it rushed out the window head first and landed somewhere below on the sandy ground quickly disappearing into the solace of the night.

I held the side of my throat and waited until my wolf had come to my side before standing. I should have been more careful, I could see it in the wolf's eyes. He would tell me more of the secrets if I would keep myself in check and not court the disaster that had almost occurred tonight. I nodded my head in silent agreement and made my way to the bathroom to clean the wound and dress it. I stared at the mirror and fell into the vision that unfolded before my eyes.

Enemies, we are enemies, a low silent tone chanted in my brain as I watched the wolves and their clansmen.

The fires burned bright as the half-naked bodies danced in time to the drum beats. War paint covered their sweating bodies and stained them with their bloody victory. The medicine men chanted for the blessing of the Great Spirit and offered the tobacco to the four corners of the world. A wolf howled from beyond the firelight and then came bravely in to its midst. He was greeted by the warriors and given a place of honor at the council fire. Somewhere beyond the wicked dancing flames two red eyes glared back, eyes filled with something akin to hate but closer to curiosity. Enemies separated from birth by their senses.

I woke up in the floor, staring at the white ceiling tile and listening to the water as it ran in the ceramic basin. I don't know how long I was out but I do know that I remembered every detail of the vision the wolf had given me. A vision of a barrier that was not to be crossed, a barrier that stood between me and the answer to my past and my future. A barrier that I would break.

Night fell in silent shrouds and brought with it a slow tantalizing aroma of sea washed breezes and pina colada. The heavy scent of coconut suntan oil had faded to a warm enticement and the lobster backs had retired from the beaches. I strolled along the slowly cooling sand digging my bare toes into its shifting surface, searching for the evaporating heat. The wind caught in my hair and sent it billowing out behind me in a streamer of black pressed against the last violet blushes of twilight. My wolf came jogging up the beach to fall into step right beside me, moving as if we were the same being.

I saw if before I actually got close enough to make it out as more than a speck against the rolling ocean waves. The rock outcropping loomed down the beach with its roughened spine pressed like a hungry mouth against the sky's breast. I could feel the thoughts that were locked in the remembrance of the shifting sands beneath his feet as my father ran to this rock outcropping and scurried across its top to find the woman he had fallen for being attacked by her husband. I fed off these tortured emotions and stalked down the beach to the weather weary rock formation. I scaled the jagged stones as they cut into my exposed heels and scrapping at my palms and arms.

Just beyond the rise of the last rock I could see the roof of the hell that housed my father. The shining domed skylights that taunted him with freedom and beckoned to him to run from the monster that lurked behind that mask of feminine love. I had become the hunter and I sniffed the air, scenting her out among the many smells that lay virtually undetected on the salty sea air. A wave crashed against the rocks and sent a spray peppering through the swirling breeze as I leapt from the rock and landed solidly on the sand. My eyes roamed back and forth in a swing pattern and I loped down the beach to the wooden stairs and then onto the back porch.

The glass doors slid silently on their tracks as I pushed them open and entered the house. Silence greeted me as I crouched just inside the doorway and again scented the air for her. I made my way up the stairs in a skulking rock like motion that held me in the shifting shadows and allowed me to become one with them. She was in the first bedroom at the top of the stairs and I was hungry.

I opened the door with skilled ease and crept inside. She lay there in the middle of the bed much like she had in my vision quest. He was there too, drowning in his own misery, a weak and pitiful sight. He turned and saw me as I approached but before he could do anything to fend me off I was pouncing on the bed and the creature that lay beneath the silk sheets. A scream echoed once as I sunk my teeth into her neck and heard the crunch of bone. I eased up then and sat back watching her frantically clawing fingers as she looked wild eyed from him to me. Blood dripped from my mouth and landed on her face and I heard her thoughts as loud as if she had screamed them. I was the demon bitch she had seen in her nightmares, the bloody whore that had come to deliver her to hell. I snarled showing my glistening teeth and blood soaked gums.

"I am your nightmare, I am the one that you have dreamed of and now there's nothing you can do to stop me," I taunted as I spit more of her blood into her face.

My father was transfixed but when he tried to move to stop me, my wolf leapt between us blocking his progress. I turned back to the screaming woman and smiled again as the blood dripped from my chin and fell on her heaving breasts. I lowered my head and bit her cheek, tearing away the flesh and watching as the blood spurted from the wound. I loved the torture, the prolonged agony. Her hands had ceased to claw the air and now lay paralyzed at her sides.

"How do you like being helpless?" I asked as I moved off of her and stared down at the pitiful sight.

"You bitch!" she spat as she searched the room for some sort of help.

"Don't bother; no one will hear you and my father can't help you. I am what your government made me and now I'm just doing some field research. Now does it hurt when I do this?" I asked as I bent by head and bit at her chin, the flesh giving way like melted wax.

It went on for hours like that, and I took pleasure in every scream I could elicit from her. By morning she lay dead and cold and I was covered with her life's essence. It was in my hair and on my clothes and bathing me with its rejuvenating abilities. I raised my head one last time from the pulp that lay on the once white silk sheets and stared blankly at my father who had turned as white as a ghost. I raised one single brow at his horrified expression and then grinned impishly.

"Now you can leave," I said as I smiled once more and the wolf trotted out the door.

He stood there still unable to speak his mind was telling me clearly enough that he was repulsed but drawn to the power of what I had done.

"We will go to William's Point now and everything will be made clear," I told him as I took his cold hand and led him from the room, "Rest, I have some cleaning up I need to do then we'll talk."

And talk we did.

The bloody moon dipped low, slinking into the crashing sea and bathing the sky with its red gore.
Red night, sailors delight, I thought as I gazed out at the tiny ships on the sea of crimson pressed against the horizon. He stood silently absorbing all that I had told him, his gaze scanning the dying sun for some revelation to explain away the truth that had just destroyed all his preconceived notions of his life. His father hadn't been the stranger that used to denounce him in front of the holy church goers with their silent fans brushing away the heat of the summer and their Sunday go to meeting clothes. His mother hadn't been the flawless angel that could do no wrong, had instead fallen to the wiles of something other than human.

"Why did this happen?" he asked as he blinked away the vision that was clouding his brain.

"I don't know that's why we have to go to William's Point. That's why we have to find the sisters that created Gypsy and find out what they know. He will be there to answer the rest of your questions but we can't stay here. The agents will be looking for both of us and it's only a matter of time before they come here," I pressed my hand to his shoulder and felt the shudder that ran through him.

"How can I have a daughter that is eighteen?" his confusion fed its way into me through the light touch we shared.

"I am a child of blood; I was made from the samples they took from you daily. I am number one hundred nineteen to be made and I am the only one that survived. All the others have died from things as simple as the flu all the way up to a form of the black plague. I don't know why I didn't die, I suppose I am stronger than all the others but I know that I am here now because you needed me and I have freed you from the hell you were stuck in," my hand fell away from his shoulder and I felt the silent push of my wolf against my legs.

"Where did you find him?" he raised a brow at the wolf that stared up at the darkening sky.

"More like he found me, he's my spirit guide. We, you and I, are of the wolf clan. All things will be made clear in William's Point," I guided him away from the railing and back into the house to collect what clothing he wished to take with him.

"You should take some of Eve's things, they may not fit very well but they'll do until we can get you some clothes," he half smiled as he cast a disapproving eye at the worn jeans and faded tummy shirt.

The Nike's had given out finally somewhere in Texas and I hadn't bothered to find another pair. I nodded and went upstairs to find something that would come close enough to fit my frame. The room still smelled of her as I prowled through the three closets she had filled with her glorious impractical clothing, nothing suitable for a trip into the mountains. I glanced at the pristine white bed covers and remembered the taste of her blood as I drank it freely. I could feel her all over the room, trapped here like she had trapped my father. I closed my eyes and tilted my head backward as I felt the energy feeding its way into my body, her energy. I was consuming what was left of her and I raised my arms as I opened my mouth and let the victory cry rip from my throat. I was pulled in a wild abandon and I knew that the ancients were talking to me as I soared upward through the domed glass destined to vision quest again.

My soul flew with the speed of an eagle past the small sleep town to the mountains we were in search of. I spiraled farther out to the settlement that had turned into a tourist's boomtown. The hangman's tree that marked the beginning to the town limits and the weathered stone that marked the founder's grave and held the name of the town. I flew beyond the limits back past the white steepled church and it's God fearing parishioners, who were praying even now, past the solemn cemetery to the black mountains, pressed against the skeletal sky and its celestial queen. I saw a place through the mountains, a pass that held no welcome for me. It was a place of magic and mystery where the ancients talked and sometimes, like now, they came back to walk among man once more.

MICAH

I was born the seventh son of a seventh son. My father was the first generation of Rominov's born in the Americas. I cannot remember his face or the sweet fading features of my angelic mother. They died when I was a child. My oldest brother, Alexander, is my only other living blood relative. He and his wife Olivia always looked after me as if they were my parents. It was during my short stint among mortals that I met Serena.

She was a beauty that made the stars weep and the moon sulk in her sultry silks and laces. Now, she is only a sweet memory as well. A memory that torments and tortures my very soul, driving me to this path that stretches out in the rocky enclaves of the wastelands I call my heart. She was also the creature that drove me to my wormy death infested bed six feet below the surface and yet, she is the reason I have come back.

I have seen the fiery pits of hell with their flaming fingers stretching their icy nails across my soul, freezing it within me. I have tasted the brimstone and drank from the blood of the lost souls. I have suffered the fever that racked my body and the malaria that befouled blood induced in my brain. A haze of broken dreams and forgotten promises tumbled through my mind as I lay listening to the worms chewing, never ceasing, constantly gnawing at the wooden barrier that lay

between them and me. It was then that I had a vision. A vision brought
me by the bony fingers of the Reaper with his skeletal smile and hollow eyes. A vision of my death and my rising.

I was twenty-five to the day when I died. It was a time of Pagan traditions and ancient superstitions whispered about by immigrants of demons and devils. All Hallows Eve, the night before All Saints Day, a time for darkened fantasies to come to light. I was at a masquerade ball that my brother and his wife were hosting. Serena was with me since we were promised to be married in the spring. Spring, a lifetime away. A lifetime I no longer had.

My friends and family, alike, celebrated the wickedness of ancient myths and delighted in telling stories of ghosts and goblins. For entertainment they had asked a fortune teller to read palms and see the future in her crystal ball. I was never one to join in games but Serena called me perverse and said I was merely being fickle if I refused. I capitulated after her sweetly pouting lips pressed themselves against my cheek. I never was one to refuse her, the fool I.

If I had known what the hag would see when I finally sat in the stiff backed Victorian chair staring at the glowing crystal, I would have run, or worse; reacted the same. Ah, pity the poor fools that learn nothing from their past for they are doomed to repeat it, again, and again, and again.

Repetition is like a comfortable blanket we become accustomed to having until it wears thin and grows old with age. Eventually we slip through the threadbare holes and no longer have its familiarity to wrap around ourselves. The past is the blanket and the future is the same unknown terrain we find ourselves floundering in blindly.

Repetition was not what she saw in her demons crystal. Death was. Black robes of a traveler from beyond with his sickle of soul harvesting. Her face became a nightmare of twisted features, contorted by the horrors that only her eyes could see and mine were too shuttered to catch sight of.

"Death will come for you tonight in the form of a friend," she pointed a gaunt filth encrusted finger in my direction.

"If that is all you have to tell me..." I began with the cold edge of steel in my voice, "then best you save it for someone that believes in your mystical lies."

"Death will not be able to hold you, for there is one that has been slighted and plots to use you as their instrument of revenge. Beware lest ye fall into the Devil's hands and become his evil avenger, his bringer of pain and death," her voice crackled along my nerves like tiny pulses of lightning as rage welled up within me.

"If Death be my future then have at me now!" I shouted as I jumped from the chair and grabbed the crystal ball, "I fear no one!"

I flung the hated thing against the floor, mesmerized as the pieces skated across the parquet surface in so many tiny shards of silvery ice. Her shriek resounded in my ears much like the sudden shattering of the glass had and I, in my midst of rage, failed to notice how everyone now stared ashen faced at me.

"There be no pity for ye now! Ye are cursed and woe be to anyone that knows and loves ye!" she wailed, falling to her knees amongst the ruins of crystal filigree.

Outside thunder rumbled in deep tones and clouds began to build furiously, matching my own turbulent emotions.

I remember precious little about the party after that. I only remember retiring to my house after biding Serena a sweet farewell. It was there within my own sanctum that Death stalked me and struck me down with one fell swoop of his sickle. Death awaited me in the bittersweet depths of amber nectar that slid down my throat. Death pulled at my insides strangling me with his bony fists until the last breath left my lungs and my dying thoughts were of Serena's lips pressed to mine.

I was buried on All Saints Day. While the heavens wept, they lowered my coffin into the darkest recesses of mother Earth. Lowered me into the pits of death induced slumber that opened in a gapping maw to swallow me in one giant gasp. I was another tiny morsel that had been regurgitated for a time and was now being reclaimed.

I slept.

I dwelled in a deep darkness that echoed the hollowness of my soul. A darkness that embodied the sweet silence of the amber nectar as it continued to coarse through my veins. How can I describe to you my tenuous state? To be alive, yet dead. To feel my limbs, my heart. To feel the heart beating in a slow sluggish tempo. A minute thumping expanding my lungs forcing stale coffin air into my very being. Making me live within the tiny unwanted tomb of pine and black lacquer. I slept still, and listened to the heart beat so foreign in my ears that I could swear it belonged to someone else. It came to me from a distance on a crimson tide of images, riding on a white horse and its name was Death and Hell followed with it.

I was plagued and repulsed by bloody visions of a hell only the Devil could have dreamed up. My body writhed in pain as the pale horseman that was my pulse burned inside my chest and forced me to live again. Do you know that terror, sheer and uninhibited, that is inherent in one buried alive beneath six feet of rocky soil, packed down tight? Do you know the madness that burns its way into your brain as you lie there listening to the worms fighting to get into your box and eat your body? A body still alive, still able to feel pain? A body slowly suffocating from the stifling air that is slipping away into oblivion?

It came to me then, like a revelation sent from Heaven. I could see clearly above me, I knew what was going on in William's Point. I could hear them all talking in hushed mumbles and screams. I could venture into their subconscious minds and read their thoughts. It was during this time that I truly felt the sting of madness as it dipped its poisoned sword into my crawling flesh.

I screamed and pounded my fists against the satin lined lid. I tore at the fabric until my fingers bled and still no one answered. What manner of person could harbor such an unbearable hatred for me? Who had I wronged so grievously? Slowly, through the miasma of insanity that had lapsed my brain I heard the soft subtle laughter, faint at first but grown stronger. It was a laughter I had heard many times before and knew too well to forget.

I froze as I listened to the soft feminine sounds as they echoed in my ears. Serena. Sweet Serena. Her image welled before my eyes and I was again transported to my time above this Earth. Her smiling face was gazing upon another, however. His dark head was bent as he whispered in her ear and invited her to dance. Not even cold and she was already in the arms of another. I dared not believe what my eyes were seeing but the pale horseman knew and my pulses leapt with hatred and anger.

I beat until blood streamed down my arms and my fists were bruised as the scene continued to play through my mind. I knew this person but could not identify him and I knew she was already in love with him, I could feel it. A dagger slicing through my stomach could have hurt no worse. It was through this din that I heard it, the faint subtle scratching from above. Something was clawing its way through the rock and soil to me. Something or someone had heard my cries. I returned with a renewed sense of purpose to pounding on the lid of the coffin. I felt the wood splinter and crack as my fist drove upward for the thousandth time and then dirt began to sift in upon me.

A new fear gripped me, one of truly being buried alive and I fought to control this fear, to send it in a different direction. Adrenaline shot through my veins as I dug towards the surface, holding my breath as dirt pressed against my face and lips, filling my nose. Just as I thought my last breath would be stolen by the shifting dirt, I felt the stony hand that gripped my wrist, pulled me up towards the moon silvered night. That was the last thing I remembered before I blacked out.

I don't know how long I lay there beneath the full moon. I gasped for air like a fish out of water, feeling each new inhalation cleanse my lungs of the foul air that had been trapped inside the coffin. When I opened my eyes it was to stare up into the face of an angel made of marble. I searched the long shadows for the person or creature that had helped me from my tomb and yet I could not see them.

As I lay there, gasping for air, I realized that the angel above me was no statue at all. She was in fact watching me, waiting for the realization to dawn. Her nails were caked in the very dirt she had dug me from. She stood perfectly still and watched as I floundered from the hole I had still been laying halfway in.

I staggered to my feet as a tear slipped down her smooth alabaster cheek and streaked its way into the low décolletage of her attire. Not a word did she speak but I could see her thoughts. Pity, remorse. I stood before her, a shabby dirty wretch. I felt like a beggar as I held my hand out in supplication to her, touching her smooth cheek and chasing away the translucent tear.

"Diamonds that sparkle in moonlight would be no less grand," I murmured as I marveled at the tears that stained my hands.

A breeze rustled through my hair as I was drawn forward by an unseen force, leaning in to the cheek of this beautiful creature. Her hand delved into my hair as I let my lips trail across her cheek to her mouth. Full lush lips flowered beneath mine, warm and inviting. Her other hand delved into my hair as I intensified the kiss and marveled at her vivacity.

Her lips left mine and trailed along my cheek to my neck. A string of warm kisses followed as she tilted my head to the side. I felt her teeth sink into the soft flesh of my throat and I moaned.

Fangs, like a snake's, sank deeper and deeper into the soft part of my shoulder, drawing from the very life that had almost been denied. The pale horseman beat fiercely as she pulled against it and the rest of my strength. I fought with all my might but was unable to break her grip. She finally let me go minutes before I would have been drained and then smiled a bloody smile at me as I fell to the ground at her feet once more.

"Drink and enjoy a life that was denied to you or return to the Earth from whence you just crawled," her subtle whisper was like butterflies wings.

Her sweet scent filled my head as she knelt beside me and bit into her own wrist. She pressed at it for a moment to make the blood surface and then pushed it against my dry mouth. I was dying of thirst, had been for days now, and this was better than the sweet nectar that had laid me low. I grasped her wrist in both hands and began to feed, starved for any kind of nutrition. A moan was torn from her throat and I cast my eyes upward to find the look of ecstasy that chased across her moon

washed face. I was filled with the same overpowering emotion as I continued to feed from her open vein. Finally she could
stand no more and shoved me aside where I lay breathless and panting.

She stared at me with those dark eyes and I could feel the heat that emanated from her as surely as I could feel the blood pulsing through my veins now.

"My debt to the Wynn's has been repaid. Your line will continue. Your brother must sire the next generation. You are now the guardian of your family and must stop at nothing to protect it. The plot that placed you in this ground was but the beginning. Do not trust her, she is no better than the poison that was so lovingly fed to you. Farewell my sweet Micah, we may as yet, cross paths again," she whispered as she ran one dirty hand through my hair.

I lay back and closed my eyes as the night wind whispered against my overheated forehead.

When I reopened my eyes the harsh light of the sun was a razor slashing through my pupils. I raised my hand to shield myself from the stinging rays and looked about for some kind of bearings. Had I dreamed the entire thing? Surely I must have. The bells in the church steeple were tolling out for service and I certainly couldn't miss that. Sweet Serena, they were probably worried sick about me. Alexander must have given me something more than just the traditional punch Olivia preferred for their parties.

I stood and dusted myself off, then left the cemetery and proceeded round to the entrance of the church. Service had already begun but I was sure I could slip in the back and find a seat amongst my family. I wasn't prepared for the way the minister's eyes rolled back in his head or the way the women began to scream as if they had just seen a ghost. Dear Olivia simply fainted in the pew beside Alexander and someone began praying for the Devil to relinquish his trickery.

Alexander was the first to approach me. He stood in the middle of the aisle and eyed me warily then walked around me as if to size me up. My eyes followed his slow progress and then he came back to stand in front of me. One hand came out to clasp my shoulder and shake me slightly then I was embraced in a bear hug that took me by surprise.

"It's nice to see you Alex," I clapped him on the shoulder then proceeded to hit harder until he finally let me go.

"You were dead," he spoke clearly as he relinquished me.

At this point in time I remembered nothing of my death or my rising and I was genuinely worried about the health of my brother's mind.

"Are you feeling well Alex?" I asked, guiding him to one of the pews.

"Better now that you are back. I don't even want to ask how this miracle came about, I simply want to enjoy the fact that my brother lives. We will have a celebration feast at my house, everyone is welcome to come join in," he shouted as he slapped me on the shoulder again, almost knocking the breath from my body.

The parishioners stared wide-eyed at me as Alexander continued to spout on about his recently returned brother. I admit I was less than coherent about anything he was saying and I seriously began to doubt everyone's sanity. Cautiously they made their way back around me, then the newly revived Olivia fell to her knees and praised God for the miracle he had wrought right before their very eyes. At the first tones of her loudly praising words sent to Heaven, the rest of the parishioners fell to their knees as well and sent up a thankful prayer for bringing back the last of the Rominovs.

I stood in the midst of these happy, tearful people and wondered what had happened that everyone was continuing to blather about. Ah, my mind was not what it had been before the grave and now it seemed as if I had been addled terribly. I was hustled off from the church back to my house and then bathed and dressed properly. The women of the town stopped by with food to fatten me up since I had now grown gaunt and thin from the week of starvation I had endured.

My brother sent a coach around for me at the time of the feast and I was amazed by the lavishness of the turnout even though they had had little to no time to prepare. I was made welcome and I felt as if I had been away for years. It was near the first tones of eight that she came in. Dressed in a red silk gown with black lace trim, she was a breath of fresh air compared to that which I had been forced to endure. Serena was as sweet as a flower as she stood in the doorway scanning the crowd anxiously. When she spotted me, I saw in her eyes a look that I had never seen before. I knew not what it meant but I cared little for the paltry trifles. I knew that my sweet Serena was in attendance and all was right with the world.

I took her in my arms and pressed kiss after kiss upon her cheeks and lips as she clung to me. A most unseemly scene I assure you but I did not care. I breathed deeply of her fresh woman's scent and knew a moment of pain in my heart as a shadowy figure of what had happened passed behind my eyelids. The specter of alabaster skin and long flowing hair as a shadowy figure pulled me from my grave. My heart stopped in that moment then raced as if the Devil himself has just arisen from the middle of the dance floor. I shoved away from her and tried to regain my composure yet the image continued to linger in my brain before it slowly faded like the tender death of a rose. On the whisper of wind that blew through the thin muslin curtains from the French doors I heard the silent promise of the night before.

Do not trust her, she is no better than the poison that was lovingly fed to you.

I could feel my dark angel's eye hidden in the darkness beyond the garden doors. I felt her pull as surely as the ocean feels the moon's. I strode to the patio and stared out across the gardens to the tree line, unaware of Serena's presence beside me.

"Now we can be married my love," Serena pressed her body against my back and hugged me tightly.

My heart fell with those words. How could I continue this charade? I could not prove the words that had been uttered to me the night before. I wasn't even sure that I had really heard them. Surely it had all been a delirium brought on by the ordeal of being buried alive. After all I had dug myself out of the grave, had I not?

"If you wish it, why don't we marry now?" I asked impulsively.

Serena stepped back surprised, I am sure, by the abruptness of my statement, "Are you sure you are well enough?"

"I am as well as I have ever been. I do not know what

happened but I do not wish to procrastinate further," I replied sounding a bit like a madman.

"This is highly unorthodox," she began.

"Unorthodox but not unheard of. The good reverend is in attendance and most of the guests are already here. Let us marry now and then we can have another ceremony in the spring if you still wish it," I took hold of her arms fighting the urge to shake her to make her see my desperate reasoning.

Her capitulation was an indomitable time in coming but finally she nodded her consent. I relaxed my grip, shaking off the gloomy thoughts that had prompted me to act so rashly.

"Let us find Alex and Olivia and spread the word," I smiled brightly, all the while secretly noting the slight downturn to her pouty lips and the less than enthusiastic way her smile did not touch her eyes.

Oh yes, I knew the fiendish plot she had worked against me but I did not know who as yet had been her willing accomplice. We were married then and there, surrounded by family and friends. My murderer and I were wed together in the bonds of Holy Matrimony.

I moved her to my home, built on one of the islands in the middle of the lake. An eccentric locale I know but as it was the home that had been handed down to me I chose to live in it. It is a lonely rambling Tudor set atop the crest of the island whose bowels hide the catacombs of my family. It was the perfect place.

From the first moment Serena sat foot on the island I could smell her displeasure. She had assumed we would continue to live in the townhouse that I sometimes occupied with my brother and sister-in-law. She complained of being cut off from her town friends and the social scene, small as it was, that whirled about in William's Point. For every one of her complaints I secretly reveled in her inconvenience. I was waiting as a cat does when a mouse is tempted by a particularly large wedge of cheese. I didn't have long to wait.

The weather had grown bitterly cold as the last vestiges of November shook off the mantle of an unusually warm autumn. The first hints of winter were already evident on the mountain peaks surrounding our small town. It wouldn't be long before we would wake up to a white blanket of snow.

My health had continued to perplex the town doctor as my appetite had grown cold towards roasted foods and hearty vegetables. I began to partake of more rare meats until finally I was near starvation with my hunger. I could not stand the dead things lying on the plates. The pale horseman in my chest wanted something more. Another sustenance, that at the time I did not understand.

I suspicioned that Serena was trying to poison me again and in that supposition I was not alone. Alex and Olivia had closed up the townhouse and insisted on moving into the mansion, hiding behind the excuse that it was unbearably lonely without my company. They had settled into a wing of the house and set about keeping an eye on my murderous wife. They didn't have long to wait.

A hearty frost lay thick as a newborn snow on the ground when I was first awakened by the pains in my stomach. It was as if I had swallowed broken glass. The handsome Dr. Prue, that was Serena's family physician from Boston, had been staying at the house assisting the town doctor in his diagnosis. Serena sent the servants to fetch the man that for some time I had been considering her conspirator. I had not been incorrect in my assumption. He entered the bedroom and in the guise of medical assistance administered the deadly dose.

The poison slammed into me, stopping my heart immediately. I lay, for all intents and purposes, dead once more. I could hear them speaking in hushed tones.

"The deed is done my love. Whatever ill spirit possessed him has now been extinguished," Dr. Prue whispered as he kissed her tenderly.

Serena nodded, "Now we can finally be together, after the appropriate time of mourning of course."

"Of course," Dr. Prue agreed turning to hide the syringe in his bag.

I watched with dead man's eyes as the two lovers embraced. The dull sluggish thud of the pale horseman began again in my chest. First a small flutter as if kissed by a butterflies wings then again. My limbs tingled and bones began to crack. My eyes slid shut as my jaws ached. My incisors elongated and pushed further from the roof of my mouth. I could taste blood as it seeped from my gums where the fangs now resided. I opened my eyes again and saw the world in a new light.

The couple were oblivious to me, all the better. The metallic sweet scent of blood that coursed through their veins was as intoxicating as that of any strong liquor. I inhaled deeply savoring the smell wanting it to last forever. My stomach clenched as the hunger that had been gnawing at me for over a month finally made it clear what I wanted.

I licked my lips as I silently stood then stalked across the room. I moved with stealth born of a predator and my prey had no idea I was about to devour them. I began with Dr. Prue and was merciless in draining the man. Serena would have screamed had I not been holding her throat tightly in my steely grasp.

She fought and clawed at the hand I had wrapped around her neck but it did no good. I had finished the good doctor in less time than it took to breathe. I turned my gaze on Serena and saw her blanch pale white with fear.

"I am what you have made me. Good night my sweet Serena, may you sleep in the same Hell you consigned me to," I whispered as I sank my fangs into the throbbing pulse at the base of her neck.

"Micah!" Alex exclaimed from the door as I dropped Serena's cold corpse on the thickly carpeted floor.

I stood, bathed in the blood of murders, flushed with shame and excitement at my kill. I did not know how to explain it to my brother. Surely he would have me hung or worse admitted to the Asylum in Rain Canyon. I felt my stomach roll at the thought.

"We will bury them in the catacombs and never speak of this again," Olivia replied calmly from the doorway.

Alex and I turned to see the steely glint in her eye and knew that this was the pact we would all take to the grave. I, however, would bear the burden much longer.

THE MANSION

The mansion sat in stately splendor; Camelot revisited. The river rock foundation of the first floor supported the Tudor style architecture of the upper floors. Wrought iron fencing surrounded the property and met and ended in a massive double wrought iron gate. The gate towered above the driveway and was flanked by stone sentinels that supported the impressive weight of the gates.

Autumn leaves trembled in the chill breeze as a loose shutter banged against the northern wall of the house. No one *lived* here, no one alive at least. Ghosts roamed the halls of the dusty old mansion. Ghosts of a past as dark and shadowy as the passages that ran beneath the island it was built on. The island sat in the middle of the lake; its closest neighbor being William's Point.

The driveway rolled gently away from the gated drive down to the southern tip of the island and the boat dock. A ferry boat landing as well as a small skiff's birth stood neglected from years of vacancy. The ferry still ran just not to this end of the lake.

The hull of the half rotted skiff was still visible just above the water line. It too had haunted memories of sunny days and the happy laughter of a fair redhead and her beaux. She had smelled of fresh jasmine and had beautiful twinkling green eyes. She had been the love of the young man's life up to the day she had been murdered.

Murdered by the same towns people that had doted on her until the lecherous eye of the priest had fallen on her creamy flesh. The same priest that had taken advantage of her and called it his holy duty to drive the sins of the flesh from her body. The same priest that had spawned himself upon many of the young girls who had later visited Seth, the illegitimate son of the dead redhead.

If the small footpath that wound away from the wreckage of the skiff could talk it would tell the story of the last time the young master of the house had trod upon it. The uncontrollable weeping that had wracked him as he carried the still form of his beloved back to the house. The impotent rage that had seethed within him as the servants placed her in the library and made her ready for viewing.

His fury had been unfathomable when the only mourners to arrive were the three witches that lived in the unholy glens of the surrounding mountains. They had laid claim to the unborn child and spirited it away in the dead of night.

The next day had poured rain; the worst storm to ever hit the town of William's Point. The lake had rose as creeks and rivers overflowed their banks.

Inside the mansion, they had buried her in a quiet service in the family's private crypt. That night the grief stricken young man had stared hard eyed out over the water surrounding his lovely home at the distant lights of William's Point. His heart grew colder with every passing second.

An eerie light shone in the mountains beyond his home and he knew the witches were at work. No doubt some fiendish plot for the unborn babe they had stolen. His mind ticked furiously as he felt hatred running hot and heavy in his veins. The sudden pounding at the front door brought him from his reverie.

A pregnant silence permeated the large house as he waited for the butler to announce their unwanted visitor. The silence stretched on for an uncharacteristic time leading him to think that it was a cruel joke perpetuated by local youngsters.

It had happened in the past, many times. His ancestral home carried with it a lurid history, one that had followed it piece by piece from its original foundation in the old country. As a matter of fact the top layer of soil on the island and deep inside the crypt had come from the original foundation.

Again the loud knock sounded throughout the empty hallways, this time right outside his study. Why hadn't the butler announced this person as discreetly as he usually did? His temper still rising, he stomped to the door and jerked it open. The butler stood ashen faced in the doorway. Behind the butler a mob of people glared back at him led by none other than the very priest that had condemned his love a mere two nights ago.

Before he could utter a word, the mob surged forward knocking the butler aside. Angry hands landed on him and began tearing at him like a pack of wild dogs. They tore at his hair and his clothes as the priest shouted at the top of his lungs about how the young man had consorted with the wives of Satan and allowed them to mutilate the body of the dead redhead. The young man could not stop the laugh that bubbled out of his throat at the hypocrisy of the man.

"See how he laughs at these grievous accusations. To the pit!" the priest screamed.

He was spirited away from his home, knowing deep in his heart that he would never lay eyes on it again. It didn't take long for them to arrive at the pit. A large stake had been placed in the ground near a funeral pyre on which she lay.

"You bastards!" he shouted as the implications sank in.

They had broken into the family crypt and dug up her body. She couldn't even rest in peace because of the evil of the bible thumping tyrant now accusing him of consorting with the witches.

Jebediah stepped forward, tears glistening in his eyes and stared at the still form of his daughter. Hypocrisy was running rampant throughout the entire crowd. Jeb had been the one to allow his daughter to be ruined by the *holy* man. His sin was as great if not greater than the rest.

The young man wrested away from the hands that gripped him and fell to his knees beside the mottled alabaster skin of his beloved. She had been his world. They had planned to wed and raise the next generation of Rominovs in William's Point. Now that dream was as shattered as her poor body. Her pale skin, even now, bore the ugly proof of the stoning she had endured.

He was wrenched away from her side and taken to the stake. His hands were fastened behind his back and he was forced to watch as her pyre was set ablaze. Fiendish flames licked upwards attempting to consume her flesh. A rumble echoed around the high walls of the pit.

The mob began to murmur and looking about the pit in terror. The sound stopped abruptly and was replaced by a pregnant silence broken only by the crackle of the flames. A low groan began and then the ground shook. The floor of the pit began to tremble and twitch as many of the mob tossed down their torches and scrambled up the sides of the shallow embankment on their way to the top of the pit.

A crack formed up the length of one wall. It's fingers snaked off as it widened and massive stones fell away. The rumbling slowly subsided as dust gently shifted back through the air. A form emerged from the crevice in the rock. His long black hair swirled in the dying breeze and the length of the long black duster waved about his legs. A slow smile curved his full lips and bared fangs. His dark eyes fell upon the last of the mob and again his smile flashed quick and deadly.

He stepped from the opening in the pit's wall and blithely strode toward the congregation. He moved with all the stealthy grace of an animal of the wilds. The wind caressed his long lean legs and pressed the duster to his superb form. He ran a tongue absently across his full lips and licked at the pointy teeth that glinted in the firelight. A dark brow raised as he looked at the priest then stopped in front of the *Man of God*.

"Your fate is already sealed, for that you shall survive this night only by the grace of the unborn and the unavenged. Jebediah, your fate has been decided and shall befall you at a later time by a daughter dead yet reborn. Peter Rominov, your fate has been sealed but as you perish here, know now that I shall breathe life back into you. I will bring to you the gift of life immortal and you shall be one with my blood again. Flames shall not sear your flesh, nothing can break you. You are my blood, my line. Go bravely to your death as I wait to give you life," Micah said as he watched the valiant fight of the last of his line as the flames consumed Peter's mortal body.

Legions of Micah's followers fell upon their mortal victims. The blood that flowed from their gaping veins ran in a river as red as the water that even now bathed the body of the reborn child of the dead redhead. The bodies were tossed upon the roaring flames of the fire as the vampires danced in wild abandon about the bonfire. The priest and Jeb were held immobile, forced to witness the carnage their actions had created.

As the flames began to reach toward the heavens, Micah walked through their depths into the middle where his son was tied to the stake.

"Drink of my blood and join me in immortality," he said as he opened a vein and placed it to the scorched lips of his son.

The flames danced and leapt then died as Peter fastened himself to the pro-offered vein and drank deeply quenching the fire that burned within him. His eyes changed from a deep dark hazel to bright red. From the depths of hell it seemed, there came a loud groan then the earth rumbled and fell away in large rocks. The rocks rolled down the sides of the cliff, falling into the pit, smashing the dying embers of the funeral pyre and scattered the coals to the four winds. Her charred flesh lay, smoking and smoldering as Peter raised his dark head, blood dripping freely from his gapping maw.

A snarl curled his handsome lips as he leapt from the last of the dying flames and lopped to the body of his beloved. A feral animal spirit had entered his soul. He was no longer the innocent young man pining for his lost love. He was now an avenger; a stalker of death; an avenger. He threw his head back and let out a howl of fierce vengeance mixed with the all too real pain he had felt as a human.

The howl ricocheted off the walls of the pit wildly and then found an answer as a pack emerged from the darkened shadows of the cliffs edges. They numbered twelve in all. Their red eyes stared down at him as they curled their lips in a feral grin then threw their heads back in unison and answered his mournful howl. The eerie sounds mixed with the night and drifted down the mountainsides towards the lake, the house, and ultimately William's Point.

Peter gathered up her broken body and lopped off toward the interior of the cave opening. His intent was clear. If she could not rest in her rightful place in the crypt below his home he would take her deep beneath the earth to the ancient salt mines where she would become the thing they had all dreaded in their nightmares. She would wait until her reborn son summoned her forth from the primordial earth to avenge her death and ultimately his as well. Until that time, Peter would command his pack and wait for the woman that would come to do final battle with the evil that still slumbered deep within the pit, hidden away from William's Point and all its inhabitants including his father and the Witches Wynn.

Micah watched as he lopped off with his dead fiancée into the welcoming darkness. Pride swelled in his chest but he was also perplexed. His dark gift should have created a creature of beauty, a child of Kane, instead Peter had become something else. Something darker and more sinister than Micah had suspected. A frown creased his fine brow and tugged the corners of his mouth downward. Something was amiss. He had become an enemy and yet he was still of his blood. How could that be? Micah would have to think on this. Maybe he would pay a visit to the Wynn's and see if they had had a hand in this.

His mind wondered back to the source from which his own immortality had come. Her cool alabaster skin, so cold and unyielding bathed in the ghostly moonlight. Her eyes shining like stars as she gazed upon him just before sinking her teeth into his neck. She had saved him from a slow death buried beneath the ground by the traitorous woman he had later married.

Serena. Sweet venomous Serena. She had slipped the poison into his brandy and then waited for it to do her will. What Serena had not, could not have known was that his beautiful angel of the night had made a pact with the witches. She had bartered the as yet unborn soul of Seth for the sleeping potion that would slow his body so that she would have time to retrieve him from the grave. His dark angel was a bit of an oracle to be able to see into the future and know that there would be a child born from a fall from grace.

Micah had wondered, when he was alone, how she had known that there would be a child. He himself had not been able to decipher the coming of the priest and his already tainted existence. Sometimes he suspicioned that his source had set in to motion the events that even now continued to transpire. Deep within his soul he knew that she had indeed come to William's Point to wreak havoc upon them all. Why? He had not yet figured out the riddle but he would, after all he had all of eternity to find out.

THE WITCHES

Night descended in torrents of unholy darkness. The wind howled ravenously as it tried to rip the shutters from the windows. The trio huddled around the fireplace inside the sanctity of the ancient log cabin. The elderly woman studied her mending closer and blocked out the sound of the tempest outside.

"Granny, why can't I go out and catch fireflies?" the little boy asked from his place at the plank top table that served as an eating surface and his homework area.

"I told ya boy, ya don't go messin' round them woods this time of night. Now be quiet and do yer lessens afor yer Paw comes home," her voice brittle with age.

"If Paw can be out, why can't I?" he whined earning him a sharp glare from his mother.

"Yer Paw shouldn't be out either. If'n that stupid cow hadn't jumped the fence he wouldn't be. Now hush afor the witches come fer ya," Granny continued to study her mending.

"Maw, what witches is she talk' 'bout?" finally a topic that peaked his six year old interest.

"Now Jobey, mind yer Granny and do them lessens before I have to tan yer hide," her voice was soft unlike the cheese grater tones of his Granny.

Jobey pouted his lower lip out and turned back to the table. Numbers didn't hold much fascination for him though, not with all the talk of witches outside. The women always seemed to take all the fun out of being young, at least being a young boy. Even though Jobey thought he was worldly for his six years he still liked a good scary story and his Granny sure could spin them.

Heavy boot heels sounded on the porch as the wind picked up again. The two women cast wary gazes at each other as Jobey turned from his studies again. The boot stopped outside the door.

"Maw ain't ya gonna open the door?" he asked as his little brow furrowed.

"Hush Jobey. Mind your studies, ain't nothing out there 'cept the wind," she had sharpened her tone, almost to a razors edge as his Paw would say.

"They's somebody on the porch, you'd best let em in," he pouted again and then turned back to his books.

"Mind yer Maw or I'll cuff them ears good," Granny grumbled as she laid down her mending and listened closely to the wind for a second.

Outside in the distance, somewhere beyond the pool of warm light that spilled onto the sagging wood porch, a low mournful cry echoed on the chill October wind. A banshee in the woods calling out to any soul that may be lost and wandering alone, a soul it could devour whole.

Inside Granny listened to the ghostly song it sang and tried to contain the chills that whispered down her boney spine and age withered skin. The witches were up to something but she couldn't say what. They probably already had Jeb, probably done sucked his bones dry and was usin' them as powder for their fires of damnation. It brought a tear to her eye to think of her beautiful son killed at the hands of them murderin' women. They should have been gotten rid of long ago but the townspeople had been too scared to do anything to them. Afraid of what the consequences might be. Afraid of the evil they might unleash on William's Point by hacking off their heads and burning their bodies.

Well, them towns folks never had to live out here in the heart of the woods and know that your nearest neighbor was a witch. All they did was hide behind their white picket fences and shut up their windows tight when the wind came a calling. No, they didn't care on whit about the people that lived in the hollers and had to put up with the scourge of the devil. They just sat back on their high and mighty pedestals and had the nerves to call her white trash because she didn't wear diamonds to bed or ride in a convertible with her hair on fire. No, she was a simple woman with a simple family and she had witches for neighbors.

Again the boot heels echoed on the porch, pacing as if in some kind of torment. Back and forth across the rotting boards, stamping out the lives of the termites that ate at the wood in unseen masses. Stalking back and forth, furious now because of the negligent insiders who staunchly refused to open the door. Pausing only when they reached the end of the porch and then turned back for another stroll.

Shutters banged noisily as the wind whipped at them steadily, tearing at the loose hinges and beating them against the walls. A deep throated growl emerged from the darkness, working its way through the chinks in the woodwork of the ancient log house. Beyond the circle of light cast by the oil lantern, there appeared two small slits of red, glaring in.

Jobey fell back as he watched the two slits of red grow and become more of the eyes that had haunted his childhood nightmares. That was just a dream though, his Maw had told him so.

"Maw, look at the winder!" he exclaimed as he sailed from his seat over to the fireplace.

"The devil's out tonight," Granny whispered as she stood up and crossed herself then spit on the dust caked floor.

"Lordy help Jeb!" Maw wailed as she crossed herself and spit too.

Jobey followed suit but wasn't sure why. The evil eyes gleamed in the glow of the lantern and seemed to bob up and down as if suspended on rubber bands. Jobey wanted to cry but at six he was a little too old to be a cry baby. Least that's what the ten year olds at school told him.

"But Paw's out there," he croaked as the eyes danced gleefully just outside the window pane.

"Yer Paw probably ain't in this world n'more son," his Maw's voice was teary as she squeezed her son close.

"Neither's that cow," Granny grumbled as she stared at the bobbing eyes and made another sign.

"Why don't them witches go away?" Jobey tried to sound brave but his voice was watery despite his strength of will.

"They won't go cause that's their master, the Devil hisself. Until he leaves, they won't either," Granny hissed as she stiffened her back and moved toward the window.

"What are ya doin'?" Maw practically yelped as she jumped back and watched Granny move toward the eyes.

"I'm gonna cast the Devil out, send him packin' and I don't mean no maybe," Granny called from over her frail shoulder.

Jobey watched spellbound as granny took the salt from the table and began to pour it at the base of the window sill. The eyes jiggled as if they were the orange jell-o they sometimes served them at school. Yep, it reminded him of the jell-o as they wobbled and quivered and then came to a shaking stop.

"Get out Satan, leave this house. We don't want none of yer kind around here," Granny shouted as the wind began to beat the sides of the house again.

It whipped down the chimney and rattled the panes but all the while Granny stood her ground. Singing hymns that Jobey only heard on Sundays from the bank of the creek while he was fishin'. He hadn't even known that Granny knew the songs that the parishioners sang in the little white clapboard church in the middle of town. Hadn't even known she was religious like them. Oh sure, Granny read her bible, read it every evening but Jobey hadn't thought of that as being religious. He thought they were supposed to show up and strut about the churchyard instead.

"Begone Satan and don't ya come round here n'more!" Granny shouted in a voice bigger than herself.

The eyes spit and sputtered for a minute then vanished just like they had appeared. The wind ceased to move and the house grew silent. No birds called from the trees, no frogs croaked cheerfully in the night and no crickets sang. All was silence. Jobey strained to hear any sound, make out any voice, any tone, but there was nothing. Had Granny sent Satan away with her songs and with that salt? Jobey wasn't sure, all he knew was that he was scared, he was six and he was scared.

Boot heels fell heavy against the rotting sagging wood and then a thunderous knocking filled the tiny room.

"Elva, let me in!" Paw called from the other side of the door.

Maw rushed to the door and fairly ripped it from the hinges. Paw stepped inside and hugged Maw tightly.

"I see'd em Elva, I see'd the witches and I see'd em dancin' to the beat the band. I'll talk to ya bout it tomorra, t'night I'm too tired," he said as he slammed the door behind them and barred it against the darkness outside.

Jobey went, unwilling to the small bed that allowed him to fall, each evening, into the slumber he needed. He listened for a time as Paw talked quietly with his Maw about how Bessy had wandered off this time, down into Black Ghost Holler and how he had watched them demons dancing without any clothes on. As much as Jobey wanted to listen he was even more overcome with the slow slumber that claimed him every night.

The next morning Jobey dressed and got ready for school, not remembering much about the night before. Only that they had come across something he couldn't explain, something his Maw and Paw didn't want to tell him about. Grabbing his books, he stepped outside and stared at the dead chicken that lay on the porch and the blood that was painted across the log walls.

"Paw, c'mere!" he shouted.

"What's a matter son?" Paw asked as he stepped out into the glare of the sun.

"Look at the porch!" Jobey exclaimed, tears shining in his eyes.

"Ain't nothing wrong with this porch, now get goin' or you'll be late," Paw gave him a little push as he turned back toward the door.

Jobey looked at the porch and saw that the blood had disappeared but it was still fresh in his mind. Even half a mile down the road he could look back and see that the bright red painted across his front porch; and he knew they'd been marked by the witches.

INTERLUDE 1 – SETH'S BIRTH

Black mooned night fell in silent shivers of expectation as skeletal shreds of grey mist rose in emaciated specters from the warm womb of mother earth. The wind whispered through the trees and tip toed across the lake, holding its breath all the while. No birds called sweetly, no crickets chirped in celestial harmony, the absences was echoed in the absence of sound. The presences of birth from death, the cycle of beginnings and endings chased each other in delicate splendor and quite subtlety. Natures small subliminal messages of the greater scheme of things.

Time ceased to be as the thirteenth hour teetered on the verge of becoming. The whole of William's Point lay blanketed in mist and filled with the same dread that had silenced the power of nature. The pitiful little parishioners slept with not a care, unaware of the mountains they were nestled in. Farther back, in the shadowed glens and valleys, huddled inside the ramshackle cottages the mountain people stared at their blazing fires burning blue in the hearths. They had scurried through their evening chores and locked all the livestock away before twilights shadows had stretched their nimble fingers across the eastern fields.

Night had descended with all the swiftness of the Reapers scythe, cleaving the landscape in two. Darkness had been a creeping pestilence that gobbled up house after house, field after field, sitting on the mountain tops, a huge black widow spider extending its legs across the land.

The mountain people had been forewarned, they had known this night was well on its way. Helpless to stop this thing from becoming, they had taken all the precautions they could. Shutters were nailed tight with the old spikes that had been fashioned after the nails of the crucifixion then blessed year ago by the Roman Catholic Pope and brought over by the earliest the settlers of William's Point.

The fires had been built to stifle the entrance from the chimney and upon all the doors had been painted the blood of the first born lambs of the year. The fattened flesh had been left at the Gateway for the unholy celebration to come. Softly at first, the faint tolling of the church bells came across the silence then it rushed forward with all the force of a locomotive. The tolling became wildly frantic as it crashed against the doors and shutters, shaking the houses with trembling anticipation. The spell of sweet silence was broken by the crazed ringing of the bells as they tolled thirteen times and then died into an abrupt muteness.

The iron tongue hung motionless, frozen mid-strike while the bell tilted at a forty-five degree angle. The wind that had held its breath before now wailed mournfully as if it's heart were broken. The time had come for the birth and the rights of passage.

Deep within the sultry sweating walls of the cave a low moan whispered past the flickering flames. Outside the chanting of the witches rumbled on the howling wind. The blue flames of the bonfire hissed with its own life as it danced in wicked splendor, summoning forth the life that lay inside.

Another low moan rent the air as the flames burst into a spectacular shower of sparks.

The blue flames of the bonfire stopped immediately as water crashed down the mountainside, creating a new waterfall. Slowly from the innermost sanctuary of the rocky womb emerged the lithe form with cat like grace. He paused beneath the cool kiss of the rushing water as it washed away the last remnants of his crimson birth.

The wet tongue of the South Holston river flicked across his long black tresses and flowed down the sinewy muscles of silky steel. It pressed kiss upon sweet tender kiss against his hot flesh, cooling his body to normal. His amethyst eyes flashed brilliantly in the fading flames of firelight. His full sensuous lips twisted into a smile of fierce predatory satisfaction as he trailed long nimble fingers through his wet hair and then further down his body. As he stepped forward the water came to an abrupt halt, leaving behind a new cut in the mountainside and a bloody lake that steamed with the natural heat it had washed away from his naked form.

Silence fell again as he walked toward the Wynn sisters that had called him forth into this realm, his unholy mothers. Gwendolyn, the oldest, stood proudly before her son, her long blonde hair unbound and falling past her waist. Her naked form glistened pale in the low light of the glowing embers. Her angelic features shone brightly the pride she felt for her son. Her arms outstretched welcomed him into her loving embrace.

Sienna, the second daughter, smiled brightly at the son she had also helped to create as first he embraced Gwendolyn then her. His features were as fine as any ever made. Her pride swelled as he held her tight then kissed her cheek gently.

Madeleine stood proud and defiant against the black sky as her son stood before her in all his naked glory. Never had there been a man as fine as the one that had sprung froth from her conjuring. Truly she was happy that they had taken the child when offered from the original birth mother. Bastard born children were not allowed in William's Point and everyone knew it. The founding fathers had stipulated it in the laws and even in this modern time the laws still applied.

The witches Wynn had served their purpose for over two hundred years and continued to serve a purpose but their time was growing short now. Soon they would have to go back to the mountain to refresh themselves. They would have to slumber for a time before they could again walk the shaded glens and valleys of William's Point collecting their healing herbs. That was why he had come. Their son would take their place during their much needed sleep. He would learn the old ways and the healing properties of the plants. He would be their eyes and their ears while they were in seclusion.

His magnificent body moved with animalistic grace as he encircled the roaring blue flames and stared deep within its depths. Knowledge emanated from the depths of his amethyst eyes as he turned his attention to the finely sculpted hands that were his own. Curiosity mixed with the wisdom of an ancient filled his expression as the sisters surveyed their handy work. His body had been constructed from the skeletons of the noblest of the warlocks from the old country. Their conjuring had brought forth the flesh that now covered the bones with sinew and muscle and the living breathing male form that was now their son. The small fetus of the baby that had been the vessel for his living soul had been the focal point of the ritual.

"Seth," they all murmured together as he peered at them, his eyes glittering in the firelight...

NO TRESPASSING

The rusted bullet riddled No Trespassing sign rattled in the stiff breeze. Jade eyed the decaying barbed wire fence and worked her jaw angrily. She whirled around and stomped back to the laughing countenance of the bane of her existence.

"Lake Malone you are a pain in my..."

"Tsk, tsk, tsk, don't let you mama hear that mouth," Lake wagged his swarthy finger in her face.

Jade felt the urge to bite it off at the knuckle but snapped her mouth shut instead. The icy glare she shot the tall dark haired boy was matched by the sudden gust of cold air that buffeted around them. The sweet scent of ripe blackberries danced around them as they both rocked gently on their feet, swaying in the breeze like the sign.

Lake's resolve crumbled and the laughter died on his lips. A heavy sigh escaped him as his broad shoulders slumped.

"Don't be mad Jade, it's just a stupid ball."

"It might be a stupid ball to you but you know how Mikey is. He's never gonna forgive either of us," Jade softened a bit when she thought about her little brother.

Mikey had been born special and all the kids at school always gave him a hard time about it. He never let it get him down though. He always had a smile and a kind word even when the others bullied him.

The others, they were the reason she was in this predicament now. They were the snotty girls who were richer than most and doted on by everyone. They were the worst of the bullies and the fact that Lake was smitten by the ring leader didn't help. Not one little bit.

Lucy Fletcher smirked at them and flipped her pale blonde braid over her shoulder.

"Lake I'm bored, let's go to your house," she pouted with poison candy apple lips.

Jade bit back the vicious reply she wanted to spit at Lucy. Hatred simmered in her veins. Lucy was the ring leader and got everything she wanted.

"I'll come back later and help you get the ball," Lake whispered before Lucy pulled him away from the fence.

Jade watched them go, fighting the urge to beat the sense out of Lucy when she *casually* nipped Lake's earlobe and shot Jade a mocking smile. Lucy's laughter mingled with the others and danced on the breeze as they rounded the bend in the road and disappeared. The sound reverberated back from the blackberry patch mocking Jade even more.

The sign clattered like rusty laughter grating on her nerves. Growling to herself she tossed down the backpack and approached the fence.

"Jade you shouldn't go in there. It says No Trespassing," Mikey whined beside her.

"Hush Mikey!" she snapped then immediately regretted it, "I won't be long. You run on home so mom doesn't get worried okay."

Mikey's blue eyes clouded with tears and he fought a sniffle.

"I'll be right behind you, just go on home. I'll get your ball and maybe I'll bring you some blackberries too," she smiled as she wiped away one of his errant tears.

Mikey was torn but eventually nodded and shuffled off the way the others had gone. He stopped once at the bend in the road and looked back at her. Tears clearly glistened on his cheeks as he waved at her then turned the bend and disappeared from sight.

In that moment Jade both loved and resented everything and everyone. It wasn't fair the Mikey wasn't like everyone else and it wasn't fair that people like Lucy Fletcher got away with murder. If she had her way she would make Lucy as ugly on the outside as she was on the inside.

With that thought lurking in her mind and a fiendish smile on her lips, Jade slipped through the rusty barbs wincing only slightly when they drug across her arm drawing a thin line of blood. Thank goodness her tetanus shot was up to date; she didn't need lock jaw on top of everything else.

As she stood on the opposite side of the fence the world went deathly silent. It was as if she had stepped in to a soap bubble. The wind stopped and the bird calls ceased, almost as if the world were holding its breath. Jade shrugged off the uneasy feeling and took first one step then another in to the blackberry patch in search of Mikey's ball.

She wandered into the patch watching for snakes the entire time she was searching for the ball.

How far had Lake tossed the stupid thing anyway, she thought.

A faint rustling from the closest bush froze her in her tracks. Mama had always warned her that blackberry thickets attracted all sorts of wild life most of which she didn't want to run in to alone. What if it was a bear on the other side of the bush eating some of the lower berries? Now the thought of being alone in this patch wasn't such a good idea. She swallowed hard and turned to retrace her steps. She would just give up her allowance and buy Mikey a new ball. He would just have to deal with it.

Jade continued walking for ten minutes and then stopped. She should have been back to the fence by now; surely she hadn't gone that far in to the thicket. Another faint rustling came to her from one of the other bushes to her right.

Jade's heart froze. It was almost as if whatever animal it was had followed her up the other side of the bushes. She schooled her fear knowing that animals could smell it. She just had to be imagining things. She was sure the fence row was just past the next few bushes and she would be safe and sound on the other side in no time. She began to walk again trying hard to ignore the constant rustling that kept time with her on the other side of the blackberry bushes.

The prickling sensation that she wasn't alone marched up the back of her head making the hairs on her neck stand on end but she continued to try to ignore the feeling. She was just letting her imagination run wild with her. She fought down the urge to run screaming down the little pathway just knowing that something was toying with her.

There is nothing there, she kept repeating to herself as she stopped again to get her bearings.

The sun was sinking in the sky and casting long shadows across the thicket now. She nodded to herself now that she had a direction firmly in mind. Her house should just be beyond the edge of the farthest row. One of her bedroom windows looked out over the creek and the very edge of the patch on the other side. She didn't know how she had gotten so turned around but it didn't matter. Now that she knew where West was she was in good shape. Jade started to walk again, her confidence restored.

In the distance she could hear the happy gurgling of the creek as it slipped over the rocks and slid through the woods that pressed up against the boundaries of the their property. How many times had she played in the creek or even gone fishing off the small foot bridge back behind her house? A smile tugged at Jade's lips as she remembered her and Mikey and Lake catching crawdads in one of the little pools under the bridge. Or the time they caught a big fat trout that had washed down out of the old Dobbs privately stocked pond after the hard rains a couple of years ago. That was all before Lake had decided he was smitten with Lucy. Now all he thought about was kissing and making time with Lucy.

Jade sneered at the thought and was reminded again how much she despised Lucy Fletcher. The girl was just downright awful, and mean, and hateful, and...and.... Jade stopped mid stride. Her nose twitched. What was that smell? A faint scent of rotting meat drifted to her lazily on the listless breeze. She covered her nose and mouth. Where was it coming from? She looked around but still could see nothing but blackberry bushes, some towering higher than her own head.

She took a tentative step forward but the smell grew in intensity. She had to get to the creek that even now sounded louder that it had a few moments ago. She had to get to the creek before what was left of the light faded from the sky, if she didn't she would be hopelessly lost in this twisting maze of prickly bushes. What would her mama and her papa say? Were they looking for her right now? She was probably gonna get a butt whooping for this one for sure. If that happened she was gonna make Lake Malone pay for it.

Lake, just the thought of him made her blood boil. What made Lucy Fletcher so much better than her anyway? Jade set her mouth and shoved through the ever narrowing path trying to ignore the thorns that tore at her arms and clothing drawing blood with each vicious swipe. Her arms stung from the cuts which just fueled her anger with Lake for putting her in this situation. When she got home she was gonna give him *what for* as her mama always said.

Jade finally shoved her way through the last of the berry bushes and stood on the edge of the creek bank. She stopped to catch her breath and survey the quickly rushing water. The light was almost gone from this side of the thicket where the long shadows of the trees gobbled up any stray sunbeam. The murky twilight that enveloped her made her shiver as the cold embrace of the dark forest lapped against her whelped up skin. The faint sounds of laughter arrested her movements as she prepared to step into the cold rushing water.

Jade looked towards the tree line on the other side of the creek but could see nothing other than black trunks. Her house was just a little ways down the creek; she could smell the fresh biscuits her mama had made for supper along with the ham she had baked in the oven. Jade's stomach growled loudly and her mouth began to water. She raised her foot again looking for the least likely place to slip when the sound of giggling grew louder. Had Lucy Fletcher and the other snooty girls followed her? Had they been the ones on the other side of the bushes? Jade scratched unconsciously at one of the cuts on her arm as the thoughts raced through her mind. If they had she should turn around and give them a good tongue lashing.

Something seemed to whisper in her ear that she should keep going, don't look back. The giggle came again, closer now. The stench of the rotting meat grew and washed over her. Jade gagged at the over sweet stench and slipped into the creek, twisting her ankle in the process. Again the giggle echoed from the creek bank, so close this time she was sure she would look up and see the mocking face of Lucy Fletcher. Jade swiped her wet hair out of her eyes and fought against the hot tears that threatened to spill across her cheeks. How dare they make her fall in the creek and hurt her ankle?! They were just ugly bullies.

Jade turned her burning cheeks up to say just that when her breath froze in her lungs. The scent of over ripe blackberries washed over her as she glared up in to the blacked face of a bloated rotting boy. His features were as familiar to her as her own. His dull eyes gleamed beneath the blackberry runners that sprouted from his arms and head. Lake Malone had followed her in to the blackberry thicket after all. He had followed her but was now something other than the boy she had known.

Hot tears splashed down over her stinging cheeks as she stretched out her hand to touch his mottled skin. A scream tore from her throat as the tips of her fingers split and green runners shot from beneath her nails. All along her arms tendrils of vegetation began to wiggle out, the scent of blackberries overpowering her.

She crawled from the creek bed to the edge of the thicket still trying to make it to her house. If she could just get home mama would know what to do. She could feel the skin on her stomach give way as something burrowed deep within the earth. A warm listlessness washed over her as a smile curled her lips. It was like she was digging her toes into the warm earth. She breathed deep and the rotting smell was gone. All she felt was the chill of evening and the sweet scent of rain on the breeze as it rattled against an old No Trespassing sign on the fence just a few yards away.

INTERLUDE 2 – SETH'S MOTHER

Mist swirled in a thick carpet obliterating everything save the tallest of the gravestones. The old Irish Cross stood solemn sentinel in the ancient cemetery. The relief sculptures swam in the heady fog as they marched up and down the face of the closed monument. How many years had it stood? Time itself had forgotten.

No stars winked down upon this saving grace. No moonbeams lit upon its ring or even its arms. All was silent save the lonesome whistle of a far off train. William's Point was at peace or so everyone thought.

Deep beneath the briny salt beds that had once been mined, there came a low rumble. Something shifted and then subsided as the Earth separated for a precious moment to spew forth the seed of damnation. It traveled up through the old mine shaft, slowly at first trying to gain its footing. Too long it had been dormant, this foul creature of the earth.

Primordial mud oozed between its toes sucking at the soles of its bare feet. The back creaked as bones popped into place after its eternal slumber. Fingers groped and dug at slimy, algae slick walls as it neared the underground falls. Ears twitched as sound reverberated painfully at first then pleasantly as water

69

slipped by in its tiny rush toward the yawning breath of the world above.

The cavern was immense as the creature stood on the precipice and let its eyes become accustomed to this small change in light. To go straight into the world above would be folly but the need was great.

The warm scent of jasmine on the autumn crisp breeze assaulted its nose. A familiar niggling began in its brain. Somewhere in the depths of its warped mind a flash of memory sent pain shooting through its limbs. Phantom laughter echoed in its head as its limbs danced a devil's jig. It looked a demonic marionette as images bright as a noonday sun attacked its mind's eye.

Red hair the color of flame in neat curls tied back with ribbon dancing on a summer breeze. Laughter echoing joyously as the sound of distant music played. The weeping limbs of a willow tree trailing lovingly through the still surface of the lake as the tiny boat drifted on an unseen current. A man's face appeared as he laughed heartily and pulled at the oars.

In a flash the memory receded and darkness replaced it, plummeting the poor creature back into the depth of Hell. For one brief moment sadness choked it as a deep and unfulfilled longing gripped its blackened heart.

The moment was brief indeed, a mere hiccup in time and space as the creature continued to make its way out of the pit of the Earth in which it had been buried.

The flames danced blue and green. Witches fire lit the moonless night and burnt the fog away from this sacred place. Sweat trickled between his shoulder blades as he worked his conjure. Seth stared long into the wicked flames and thought the silent chant as his hands rested upon his knees.

The thick cloud of herbal incense billowed to the heavens but it was the bowels of the Earth that this spell was bound for. His magic was true, his intent real, and his energies were completely focused. The one recurring image in his brain was that of hair the color of flame in neat curls tied with a ribbon. It was how his mother had been described, how the one true picture he had seen of her looked. Laughing blue eyes, alabaster skin and the wonderful scent of jasmine.

Her things were there, the silver comb she had used to brush the tangles free. The satin ribbon of purest white. The tattered picture that had survived her body. The image smiled back at him giving no indication of her final misery and degradation.

The delicate handkerchief that all the items rested on. Small inconsequential things that were all that marked an entire life. A tiny shell found along the banks of the lake that she so dearly loved. A ragged paper from the juke joint she used to sneak away to. The music had called to her and she had gone much to her parent's chagrin. It had been the beginning of the end.

Again Seth pushed the dark thoughts from his mind and instead picked up his stone mortar and pestle. He had mixed the potion well and was ready for the final step. With the tip of the silver bladed ritual knife, he pricked the tender vein of his wrist and held it over the mortar. The blood dripped into the herb sending up the frisson of smoke he had awaited. It swirled and danced then mingled with that of the incense and fire. In the essence he made the wish; the one that stabbed in to the belly of the Earth and brought forth a low moan as if it reeled in agony.

"It is done," a disembodied voice whispered softly on the slow drifting breeze.

Seth closed his eyes and murmured the wordless chant over and over as the cut on his wrist began to heal.

ALBATROSS

In William's Point a man's sins carry from one generation to the next; an Albatross of his evil deeds on earth. No bird of good fortune, only a record of his misgivings. This omen carries with it a price. A price that is costly in the end. Death is its mistress and she takes pleasure in her work, beware the Albatross.

The hazy cloud of smoke hung thick in the air as the flames jumped higher in the old stone fireplace. The people gathered about it stared deeply into the reds and oranges that danced with all the fury of a writhing beast. Their tired old faces were lined deeply with the years of hard work that had built their characters. Outside the wind howled forlornly and pushed against the clapboard sides of the tavern. Inside their minds numb with drink they sat and waited as the one upstairs lay in agony awaiting the reaper's scythe.

A loud wail descended the stairwell as the inhabitants sat silently watching the fire. No one moved. No one blinked. No words were uttered as another pain filled wail floated down from the upper stairs of the tavern. They all sat suspended like puppets from their strings. Fixed to one point, idle with no visible signs of emotion or empathy for the dying man.

A shutter pulled loose from its hinges and swung wildly in the air as the door crashed open with a burst of wind to reveal the tall slender form of the town priest. He stepped in as a blast of rain pelted down from the blackened sky. His face was crisscrossed with lines from his years of outdoor service in a somewhat less reputable position. Even the good priest had strayed in his youth but now that was all behind him. Or so it would seem.

Again the agonized cry came from above and again it was ignored. The priest took a seat beside Old William and motioned for Jeb to bring him a draft of the house specialty. He had toiled long and hard that day, casting the demons out of the young girl Tabitha that lived with the Widow Merchant on the outskirts of town. Her creamy flesh had bore the mark of the devil and had had to be cleansed. A cleansing that he loved to dish out and the young ladies who received it often never forgot.

He could still remember the knowing look on the Widow's face as she left him alone with the girl. Tabitha had run away from William's Point on her eighteenth birthday. She had engaged in illicit sex with men and had been branded by the devil when she came back to William's Point. It had been rumored that she had been seen with the demon spawn that the witches had brewed. If that were the case then the carnal knowledge the priest had gained from her mattered not for her soul damned to the hell fires of Satan's minions.

Seth, the witches' bastard offspring, lived in the mountains and was the walking proof of the evil that dwelled in the pristine community of William's Point. His presence would soon have to be dealt with but right now there were more pressing matters at hand. Such as the one upstairs at this very moment. The priest turned his bleary gaze up as rushing footsteps echoed on the old planks that served as ceiling to the inhabitants below and floor to the ones above.

"Send for the doctor," the ruddy faced young barmaid called down the stairwell as she ran for the kitchen at the back of the bar.

"There's no time for that now," the stout, pig faced bartender growled as he caught her arm and squeezed it tightly.

Her eyes swung round and saw the black clad figure seated at the bar and noted the dying flush of sexual gratification that even now marked his hideous face. A shiver of cold ran through her as she remembered those filthy old hands on her body, swearing to all those around her that she had been marked by the devil. Five years and the memories were still as fresh as if they had happened only moments ago.

"What's that bloody bastard doing here?" she mumbled as she tried to free her arm from the beefy fingers that still held her.

"Mind your tongue girl. He is a man of God and your elder," Jeb growled again.

"He's no man of God if you ask me and he is definitely not worth my respect," she spat as she finally succeeded in freeing herself from his grasp and tumbled onto the kitchen floor.

"You'll do as I say or out with you," Jeb said as he followed her into the kitchen and stood menacingly above her prone form.

She threw a protective arm up as Jeb raised one of his big clubs of a fist to clout her in the head but the blow never came. The action was stopped by the sound of the front door crashing in again and another gust of freezing rain rushing into the room. All eyes turned from the prone figure of the barmaid to the open door as the stranger stepped inside and shook off the raindrops that clung to the huge black cloak that was wrapped around the newcomer's body. The fresh scent of jasmine rushed in on a gust of raindrops.

"Bar's closed," Jeb barked as he left the girl lying on the floor and returned to his post.

The hood of the cloak fell back to reveal long glossy red curls that tumbled down and around the small white face of the female that had just entered the establishment. Her blue eyes shone brightly as she glanced from one inhabitant to the next, all mindless sheep waiting for the slaughter. One eyebrow rose as if to question the bartender's words but no sound escaped her lips.

"Can't you hear? The bar's closed," Jeb said again, slightly unnerved by the look in the girl's eye.

"I'm not here for you," the stranger's softly spoken tones stilled the sudden tumultuous bleating of the otherwise silent patrons.

A murmur rose like a wave and resounded around the room as a distant clap of thunder rocked the foundation of the building and a cry of agony ripped through the upstairs. Her eyes turned upward as lightning lit the sky behind her and cast her face into a series of strange shadows. For a split second, the image of a skeleton seemed to float into the room directly behind her. The ghastly image of death disappeared as quickly as it had entered.

The priest turned and stared at the beautiful woman that had glided into the room. She was a brazen one, filled with fire that shone in her crowning glory. Surely she was marked by the devil somewhere and he would find it if he had his way about it. Fiendish pleasure lit his eyes as she approached his end of the bar.

"Here now girl, don't you listen too well?" Old William dared to glance at the young miss that was dressed as if she had stepped out of time.

Her gossamer gown clung to her bodice showing the dusky areolas of her breasts from the moisture that had slipped in from the rain. A strange necklace nested between her breasts that bore a tiny silver bird, an albatross on a chain.

"You should clothe yourself better, young lady, before some of these men get notions about your morals," the priest admonished as she sat down on the stool nearest his and placed her delicate alabaster hands on the scarred bar top.

Her blue gaze slid to his, as he licked his lips and glanced again at the wet bodice of the flowing dress. Another moan, weaker now, echoed from upstairs as all the occupants ignored the sound again; their minds taking in the pathetic need for human comfort but relinquishing none. The man had made his bed years before and now must lie in it. The barmaid returned from the kitchen, meekly carrying a pitcher of steaming water. The young woman's gaze fell on the barmaid as she skittered past.

"Here now, get upstairs and shut that old fool up," Jeb shouted as the barmaid slipped past.

On her way up, her gaze locked with the newest patron to enter the bar. A chill froze her to the spot until a huge hand shoved her forward, sending the scalding hot water sloshing out onto her hand, making her yelp in pain.

"Here! Look at this mess you've made. You'll have to clean that up as soon as you get back down here," Jeb grouched at her.

The blue gaze reassured the barmaid without a word as she moved her leaden feet past the grasping hands and mounted the stairwell.

"Damn girl can't carry water in a jug without spilling it all over the floor," Jeb grumbled as he sat a beer down in front of the new arrival.

"Why don't you fire her?" Old William called out as he waved for another drink to be sent his way, ignoring the tiny twinge of his conscious at the thought of what should and shouldn't be done for the man upstairs.

"I would but her maw is in a hard way and this is the only way she can help support that idiot she has for a son. You know when that boy was born they should have taken him and not even told her about it. 'Faye,' I said, you can't support a child like that. It just ain't right. What good is he? Can't write, can't read, and can't even wipe his own nose. From what I hear, though, he's taken up the habit of peeping in on Ms. Culpepper down on the branch," he slid another rum down to Old William and stood back; spit cleaning a glass with a dirty rag.

Another moan slipped from the upstairs, wet with a wheeze that seemed to hang in the air with them, ominous as the thunder that rumbled in protest. A chill crept into the barroom as the inhabitants tried to shut out their thoughts and remembered deeds.

"Where are you from young lady?" the priest asked as he placed his big warm hand on her tiny one.

An icy glacier would have felt like a heat wave compared to her skin. She was pale as death and felt the same.

"Goodness, girl, you're freezing to death. You better take that cloak off and get warmed up. Jeb, take this back and give her something that will take the chill from her pretty flesh," he called out to the bartender as he pushed the beer back to make way for the hot toddy.

"That's what you get for running around out there in this kind of weather dressed in nothing but that garb. Why, if you were my daughter, I'd..." Jeb broke off as someone called out from the back of the tavern,

"If she was your daughter, Jeb, she'd be dressed in less!" A round of raucous laughter filled the room as the poor soul upstairs continued to moan in pain.

The memory of Jeb's daughter spread-eagle beneath so many leering eyes filled all the minds to almost hallucinogenic proportions. The image seemed to swim about the room riding on a wave of first one memory then another, leading ultimately to the time of her death when she had been stoned only a few short years ago.

"If I were your daughter, you would be dead." Her soft tone brought silence to the room again and a thunderous rage to the bartender's red face.

"Now see here, you don't need to be talking to Jeb that way. He's a good ole soul," the priest admonished as he gripped her hand tightly, and then slid his fingers down to fall below the lip of the bar.

His sins were as big as the rest of them, he too had taken pleasure in her flesh as she had cried out in rage and anger but her father had turned a deaf ear. She had consorted with the devil and had paid; they all paid in the end. She had been tragic though, pregnant and alone, she had been forced out onto the street and stoned for breaking one of the sovereign laws of William's Point...no bastard children were allowed.

His hand edged its way until he found the woman's thigh and rested there for a moment. A thrill filled his veins when she didn't move away. She was up on playing his game and that sent even more of an adrenaline rush pumping its way into his organs. He was growing harder by the minute as the soft scent of jasmine filtered from her long hair to his nostrils. She was all woman, and he was more than willing to warm her cold limbs with the heat of his labor.

The air was filled with the last spasms of the agony from above. The death rattle had begun and it would only be a matter of time.

"Why doesn't anyone go to see about the man upstairs?" She asked as her blue gaze settled on the 'holy' man that was even now trying to find a way to run his fingers along her bare flesh.

"He is a sinner that is paying for his time here on earth. Death will come for him but his pain has only just begun, from your necklace I see that you are familiar with the legend of the Albatross. What sins do you harbor my child?" the priest purred diminutively as he let his fingers search for a hem or some kind of opening to the strange antiquated dress.

"Death has come for him and you all," she smiled demurely as she stood from the barstool and glided to the stairwell.

"What the hell was that supposed to mean?" Old William asked as the girl disappeared from sight.

"Weird girl," Jeb grumbled and spat into another glass then began wiping it with the greasy rag, all the while trying to shake the strange feeling of deja vu.

The hallway was barely lit by dim bulbs that had probably been there since the beginning of time itself. The young woman glided down the corridor never faltering, never pausing in her pace. Her destination lay at the very end of the hall and she was well aware of the pain on the other side of the door.

The barmaid opened the door intuitively, as if she had heard a knock, but the woman had neither moved nor appeared to be walking on the floor. Her feet, although not visible to the naked eye, seemed to hold her off the floor. The barmaid stepped aside as the silence communicated the woman's wishes louder than words.

The old man lay in the midst of the bloody sheets, a sweating mass of misery and pain. His eyes were glazed over from the torment of his hemorrhaging body. The bed linens were stale and the parts that weren't crimson were grey with filth.

"Who's there?" he whispered, weak from the death struggle.

"Someone who has come to take you home," the barmaid answered as she moved to stand beside the shining figure in flowing white and black.

"It's finally over," he whispered as she took his hand.

The woman held tightly to the fragile life force and the barmaid watched as it began to ebb away before her very eyes.

"Before I'm gone I have to tell you something.....listen close and I'll tell you why I shot the Albatross...the bird sent to plague me through life. I must repent my sins; give them to the next generation. I have murdered one that is close to me. One that no longer sees this world with her eyes. I have done thee wrong fair and beautiful lady by forcing myself upon these pale alabaster hands, this cool flesh of womanhood. I have taken what you did not offer and I have paid for it throughout my living hell as those, my peers, set listening as I die. I have killed my Albatross, my beautiful sweet bird," his feeble words dripped into her ears, the last dregs of the nectar of his life, "It was my stone, the last to be cast that took your life and set your son onto the path he is now on, forgive me my trespasses as I have forgiven those that wait for my death sentence. I, too, am a lost soul set upon a path not known to me. I knew it would be you that came for me. I only ask that you take them as well....the last wish of a dying man....send me not into redemption without the knowledge of their punishment."

The barmaid listened as he spilled out the sins of his soul, and then slipped away into the night with the woman. Her eyes brimmed with sorrow as she gathered the pitcher and what few rags remained that weren't covered with blood. Her mind whirled as she realized she had just heard the confession of a killer. Jeb's daughter had died seven years ago to the day and in that time all had known that she was stoned for breaking the law. Women lived in fear of the old laws still held in force by narrow minded officials that thought it added a sense of tradition to William's Point.

Exiting the room, she felt a warm breeze as the image of the woman reappeared again in the hallway.

"You showed an ounce of human kindness and for that you will be repaid. Go downstairs and collect your things, then leave this place. I, too, must slay the Albatross, I must remove my sin. Never look back." Then the woman was gone, leaving behind only the soft scent of jasmine.

The barmaid turned and ran down the stairs. She collided with the solid chest of Jeb and fell to the floor. Fright filled her eyes and racked her frame as she fought to regain her footing and get out of the bar.

"Where do you think you're going?" Jeb demanded as he sent her sprawling again and tossed a mop in her direction.

"Is the old fool dead?" Old William asked as he turned up the last dregs of the rum.

She nodded in dumb confusion as she stared from one face to the next and saw the skulls gleaming brightly beneath their flesh. Every lascivious thought ever to cross their minds pounded in her brain as she fought to keep from screaming. The images of their molestation of the young woman she now knew was Jeb's dead daughter sprung to her mind as she remembered the filthy priest's hands touching her as they had touched the wraith upstairs. A spirit come back to take its revenge upon the living.

"You been struck dumb or something, girl?" The priest asked as he reached for her and was chagrined as she shrunk away.

The room fell silent as the two figures appeared at the top of the stairs. One was the floating figure of the woman that had carried in the scent of jasmine. The other was that of the skeleton that had slipped in behind her during the lightning flash. In their hands, they carried a pair of die and cast them upon the floor; they tumbled with deadly clarity down the stairs and rolled to a stop beside the barmaid, echoing in the thunderous silence.

"Snake eyes. I have won," she called out to the inhabitants of the bar. "You all belong to me now." She smiled broadly as she read the bones and motioned to the inhabitants of the bar as a whole, "I shall have you as you had me, spread-eagle beneath my ravenous gaze. Your souls bared, your teeth gnashing, your bodies lying in torment and torture. I shall take you to Hell and burn my sins at the stake."

The hideous grin of the skeleton mirrored the woman, and then set its scythe to work harvesting.

Screams rent the air as soul after soul was pulled from their earthly vessels. Fire sprang up from the floorboards as pits opened and sucked the crying souls down. The bodies hung in the balance, tiny pendulums that swung back and forth on the scales the lady held in her right hand.

The barmaid rolled onto her side and covered her head as the horror filled her ears with the sounds of death and the stench of brimstone and burnt flesh filled her nostrils. Charred timber fell from the ceiling as the woman continued to reap the sin that had been sown. The priest stood and shouted against the devil, pounding the bar with his fists and screeching until he was red in the face.

"And you," she said as she turned to face him, "you will be my finest prize yet. You who claim to be a holy man and then feed your fantasies off the flesh of frightened women. You are mine forever and it is forever that I will kill you, again and again, my poor sweet

Albatross. No bird of good fortune but a fowl of evil hides within your heart that poisons mind after mind, body after body. Marring all you touch, seeding it will the stench of your insurrection."

With those final words, she disappeared along with the priest and the entire company. All that remained were the smoldering timbers that fell about the slight figure of the barmaid. Fires crackled and danced around her, but their flames never touched her. Her hair, once raven black, had grown white and her eyes dark as the midnight sky. No words came from her trembling lips but she possessed the strange aura of ethereal power as around her neck nested an odd necklace with a tiny silver bird hanging upon the chain, an Albatross of sin waged and witnessed. Confessions of a long dead killer and the secrets of a wraith with her deadly lover. Her dress was a gossamer gown of flowing white and a long black cloak lay next to her. The scent of jasmine hung fresh and heavy in the air.

RESURRECTION

The hulking figure of the abandoned brick school house loomed on the dark horizon lending a false sense of security to the bedraggled band of backpackers. Night had caught them at the worst possible time. It was a well-known fact to all hikers that travelled the trail that one simply did not wish to get caught in the area around William's Point, especially after dark. It was the subject of whispered conversations late at night over the dying embers of campfires. If you travelled that way you had to plan your time wisely to make sure you passed the town during the bright light of day and even then you prayed you weren't the next one to go missing.

"Dammit Morgan, why did you have to take so long at the last stop? Now we have to either keep going or take shelter," Sasha complained as she nervously eyed the open expanse of field.

The only shelter to be had was the abandoned school house.

"Seriously Sasha are you a big 'fraidy cat?" Morgan taunted as the other guys chuckled.

They had all hooked up at the last trail shelter and agreed to go this leg of the journey together. Sasha knew Morgan was just trying to cover up his own misgivings about this area but she didn't care for his manner. Her slitty eyed glare said as much but unfortunately the affect was lost in the overwhelming expanse of blackness that was settling even heavier around them.

It was a new moon and not even the stars were coming out to play. The inky blackness had obliterated the horizon and was quickly gobbling up the outline of the old building.

"Knock it off Morgan, I have to agree with Sasha," Quin said giving Morgan a quick shot to the arm.

"Yeah, yeah, yeah," Morgan growled, "let's just go. We can keep walking."

"Right and run up on a wild animal or worse fall in a hole and break a leg. I don't think so Morg, we're gonna have to stay in that building for the night. Let's just hope there isn't some disgruntled farmer that comes out and shots us," Tristan piped up and shoved Morgan towards the crumbling ruin.

It was on the tip of Morgan's tongue to disagree when they heard the far off cry of a wolf.

That couldn't be right; there weren't any wolves in this section of Virginia. Maybe it was a coyote, Morgan thought as he reluctantly began to trudge towards the old building.

Another mournful howl answered from the opposite side of the field. The tiny hairs on Morgan's neck rose and stood at attention as his heart faltered for a moment. A third howl answered this one from their right. A few seconds later another howl responded from their left. Holy crap! They were either surrounded or that mother was moving quickly.

"Get your ass in gear Morgan," Sasha hissed as she began walking a little quicker towards the lesser of two evils as far as she was concerned.

"Who the hell builds a school house in the middle of nowhere?" Tristan asked not expecting an answer but trying to break the tension of the group.

"Don't know and don't care right now. I think I would probably kiss them if they were here right now," Quin said as the brick walls loomed closer.

The haunting sounds of howls grew closer with every step and it wasn't long before everyone in the group knew the animals were keeping pace with them. Morgan began to sweat and fought the urge to break out into a run. That would be the worst thing any of them could do at this moment. It would signal the pack that they were prey and the dinner bell had been rung.

"I swear they must be so close we could see them," Morgan breathed as he kept his eyes on the broken windows ahead of him that were just now glinting in the beam of their flashlights.

"Just keep walking, we're almost there," Sasha replied as she hitched her pack a little higher on her shoulders and kept walking.

The school house was a considerably large two story building standing on a gentle rise in the middle of the vast open field. A crumbling set of moss covered stone steps lead up to a dilapidated fence that half-heartedly surrounded the school yard. If it had been the middle of the day Sasha would have been the first one of them to say *let's go exploring*, as it was she would rather be anywhere but there at that moment.

Rusty hinges squealed in protest when they pushed the wrought iron gate open to enter the school yard. A low growl rolled across the field behind them and the urge to run took over. All four of them sprinted up the rotting steps to the porch then slammed into the old oak door.

"Don't let it be locked, don't let it be locked, don't let it be locked," Tristan was saying as he pounded up the stairs behind the rest.

The door gave way when Tristan slammed into their backs and they all tumbled inside. Quin kicked out violently, slamming the heavy oak door shut behind them. They all jumped up and sprinted through the rooms to check out the windows.

"This room is okay," Tristan called.

"So is this one," Sasha shouted back.

"They all look like they've been boarded up on this floor," Morgan replied as he came back from one of the back rooms.

"Well, I'm not complaining," Quin replied as he checked the oak door to make sure it was going to hold fast.

Silence reigned inside and out, but the overwhelming feeling of eyes watching crawled across Sasha's skin as sure as if someone else was there. She rubbed her arms trying to shake off the feeling and get rid of the sudden bout of goose bumps that marched up and down her exposed skin.

"What the hell do you think that was out there?" she asked.

"Probably coyotes or wild dogs, in either case you don't want to get caught out by a pack and that was exactly what that sounded like," Quin replied as he gave the door handle one final shake then turned back to look at Sasha's ashen face.

The girl was visibly shaking but she was holding up pretty well. She had told them that she was from somewhere out west and had started hiking the trail on a dare from one of her friends. They hadn't thought she would make it a mile before she chickened out and turned back or called for someone to come and get her. So far she had proven them wrong. Quin admired her for her grit and how she had stuck it out. From everything she had told them Sasha was a pretty pampered girl back home. To look at her you wouldn't think she had grown up in a mansion in Beverly Hills.

Her long blonde hair was tied back in two braids and the old worn out red bandana covered the top of her head. Her natural California tan had deepened because of her time on the trail and not to be too ungentlemanly she wasn't the cleanest one out of all of them. She had taken a tumble the day before she met them and was still sporting the mud splatters and some pretty nasty bruises.

Quin had felt protectiveness towards her the first moment he looked at her big brown eyes and saw that she wasn't expecting a hand out from anyone. She had a stubborn set to her jaw and an attitude to match. He guessed she had a chip on her shoulder but she hadn't acted that way towards them, well; except maybe Morgan. She and Morgan seemed to enjoy taking jibes at each other.

Morgan, now there was a peculiar person if Quin had ever met one. One minute he was Mr. Jokeman the next he was sullen and withdrawn. For the most part he joked and kidded around but sometimes Quin just didn't know how to interpret his humor. He and Morgan and Tristan had all met up somewhere on the first leg of the trail and had hit it off pretty good. They had decided since they were all going to the summit they would all go together so they had been hiking as a trio since then. It was a good thing too because they had heard more and more stories the closer they got to this particular leg of the trail.

Tristan pulled his pack off and dropped it in a corner pulling Quin's attention to him. Tristan was like the little brother to all of them. He had sandy brown hair and a surfer dude attitude. He was from Florida and had decided to hike the trail during his break before he started college. He was going to become a Marine Biologist but instead of spending all his time in the ocean he had decided to go overland. The fact that it might take seven months to finish the trail hadn't deterred him any. He would just start his classes in the spring.

Quin shrugged out of his own pack and dropped it beside Tristan's. He rubbed a hand across his face and stifled a yawn. It had been a long day of walking and he was tired even with the jolt of excitement they had just experienced.

"We better get comfortable and try to get some rest. I imagine that those dogs will go on now that they know we are out of their reach," Quin said as he glanced around the wide open hallway.

It was his first real look at the place. The old floorboards were still solid beneath his feet. The walls had aged and the paint was peeling but they were just as intact as the floor.

"I wouldn't stir up much dust if I were you, it's probably lead based paint," Morgan took the words right out of Quin's mouth.

They all solemnly nodded as they began to inspect their surroundings. A wide staircase dominated the middle of the hall and lead to the upper floors of the school.

"This must have been one helluva school house," Tristan said as he wandered over to the first door and opened it in to what must have been the administration area.

"We should probably pick a room and try to get some rest," Sasha said as she picked her pack up and peeked around Tristan into the cavernous office area.

"I agree," he nodded and went back to pick up his pack.

There was a loud thud as something slammed against the door. Dust shook free but the old hinges held. All of the occupants jumped and stared at the door.

"I think we need to head up instead of staying on this floor," Morgan's voice wasn't as sure as it had been before.

"That sounds like a good plan," Quin replied as he motioned them to precede him up the staircase.

He kept his light fixed on the old oak door as another thud made the door shudder but it still held fast. Shit! Whatever had chased them inside was now trying to break down the door. Coyotes and wild dogs didn't do that! Quin swallowed hard and moved up the wide expanse of stairs trying to keep his eye on the door but make it safely up the steps at the same time.

The blackness was all encompassing at the top of the staircase. The rooms were deep wells of darkness filled with row after row of old wooden school desks and aged blackboards. It was as if everyone had simply filed out at the end of the day and never returned. Moldering books lay open on top of some of the desks, left at the same page that the last human eye had been reading.

A chill ran up Quin's back as they moved through this monument to a past that was caught somewhere in time. He could almost hear the patter of feet on the old plank floor boards and the whispers of children's voices as they passed each empty room.

Easy old boy, it's just your imagination, he thought to himself as he turned quickly thinking he had seen a shadow of movement out of the corner of his eye.

"Are you okay?" Sasha asked as she fell into step beside Quin.

"Yeah, just a little jumpy about how dark the building is," Quin mumbled as he tried to make light of his angst.

"Down this way, looks like it must have been a library," Tristan said from somewhere to their left.

Quin could barely make out the tiny spec of Tristan's headlamp in the gloom of the hallway.

"How big is this thing?" he mumbled more to himself than Sasha.

"It must be massive. Can you imagine what it must have been like to go to school here?" Sasha whispered.

Quin nodded reflecting that the building seemed to be holding its breath, no wonder Sasha was whispering that was how he felt as well. They caught up to Morgan and Tristan as they lingered in the doorway to the old library. Good heavy doors stood on silent hinges.

"This should be a good place to hold up for the night," Quin nodded as he surveyed the doors and then nudged one gently.

The door swung shut silently. He exhaled and felt the first ray of hope. He looked around the inside of the library. There were several low heavy bookshelves that they could shove in front of the doors.

"Let's move some of those shelves over here in front of the doors just to be safe," he murmured and was surprised when Morgan dropped his pack and put his back into it.

Sasha helped them shove another bookcase in front of the doors then stepped back. The room was stygian dark. The library must be one gigantic cavern from the looks of it. Her headlamp couldn't even illuminate the back of the room. Everywhere she looked she found old books left lying helter skelter. Her skin crawled as she felt a thousand tiny eyes watching her even though they were the only inhabitants of the room.

Chairs still sat around rickety tables the tops littered here and there with old papers and discarded books. The air was thick with waiting silence as if the abandoned building were holding its breath in anticipation for the first domino to fall. Sasha wondered what that domino would be then chided herself for even entertaining the thought. She briskly rubbed her arms trying to stave off the chill of the abandoned building.

"I wish we could build a fire," she mumbled more to herself than the others.

Her muted tone sounded like canon fire in the pregnant silence and all of them, Sasha included, jumped at the sound.

"Sorry," she murmured then put her backpack on top of the central island that must have served as the circulation desk.

Tristan followed suit and soon all of their backpacks lay on the dusty top of the old oak desk. Morgan walked stealthily to the windows and wiped at a half broken glass pane. He shook his head, the motion barely discernible in the inky darkness.

"I can't see anything," he whispered as he turned back to the group.

"Let's hope that door downstairs holds and whatever was chasing us gives up and goes away," Quin replied as he took a tour of the front portion of the library.

Cobwebs hung thick in the corners as his light reflected off the multiple eyes of the arachnids. He hated spiders, always had, they had too many legs for his taste. He stifled the shiver that ran down his spine and moved farther back into the deserted bookshelves. They had nothing but time and he knew he wasn't going to be able to sleep.

"We should set up a guard duty, everyone taking a turn," his voice echoed back from the cavernous room as he meandered through the floor to ceiling book shelves.

How could someone have left all of this behind? There was no way this small town could have so much money as to throw away this kind of library. He played the beam of his headlamp across some of the titles and shivered again. Mixed among the common place library books were titles he didn't recognize. Books that referenced witchcraft and histories of werewolves or vampires, illuminated by his light, peered back from the ancient bookshelves. He must have found the horror section of the library. He had never had books like that in his school library.

"Hey guys I think I found something," Tristan's voice was distant as if he were at the very back of the library.

Quin made his way through the maze of bookshelves towards Tristan's voice. He had found the librarian's office tucked at the back of the library, another oddity since most librarians lorded over their domain like tyrants; at least that was what Quin remembered.

The door stood askew and Tristan looked around at his companions before reaching out to give it a little push. The door scraped along the hardwood floor like finger nails on a chalkboard. If silence was their goal they were failing miserably at it.

"Tris, you just about made me crap my pants," Morgan grouched and gave Tristan a punch to the shoulder.

"You, I think I already did," Tristan swallowed hard as he hovered on the threshold.

Sasha rolled her eyes, "Scardy cat, get out of my way."

Before any of them could catch her, Sasha ducked into the room that sprawled across the back of the room. They all cast wary looks at each other trying to decide who would be the next one to be swallowed up by the darkness. After a moment of hesitation Quin stepped forward and holding his breath ducked into the room.

The moment he stepped across the threshold he was surrounded by silence thicker than the silence in the rest of the library. He stood in the middle of the void and cast the beam of his headlamp about looking for Sasha.

"Sash, where are you? Did your headlamp go out?" he asked as he took another step farther into the room.

"I'm over here," Sasha replied in hushed tones.

He couldn't see her headlamp so she must be having problems with it. He walked in her direction and grunted when he ran into the edge of a desk.

"Watch out," she said a little too late.

"Dammit, I can't see a thing even with my light on," he grumbled as he looked down and saw the corner of the desk he had just walked right into.

"I know," she replied, "I think I found a fireplace."

"Quin, Sasha," Tristan called as he shuffled in behind Quin.

"Watch out," Quin replied but grunted again as Tristan ran in to him in the dark.

"Dammit Quin, why couldn't I see your light? You're standing right here and I couldn't see it two feet away," Tristan grumbled as he edged around the desk.

Quin didn't want to ponder on why they couldn't make out each other's head lamps; as a matter of fact Quin didn't want to be in the room any longer.

"Come on Sasha, I don't care if there's a fireplace in here or not I think we should just go back out to the circulation desk and wait until morning. We have sleeping bags, we'll be fine," Quin said as he peered in the direction Sasha's voice had come from.

When she didn't answer Quin's throat went dry, "Sasha?"

A wispy sensation skimmed along his arms as if he had just walked through a huge spider's web. Quin jumped and fell back into Tristan bating at his forearms.

"Dammit Quin, what are you doing?" Tristan asked as he fought to balance himself.

"Something just touched my arm," Quin breathed.

"You probably just ran in to a cob web."

Quin nodded even though it was a wasted effort. Why hadn't Sasha answered him? He stepped forward again expecting the brush of cobwebs but didn't encounter any. Maybe he had knocked them down before. He slid another foot forward and felt his heart freeze when the hiss and pop of a match igniting in the room thundered like a gun shot. At the far end of the room, maybe twenty feet away, Sasha lit a fire in the massive fireplace.

Quin turned off his head lamp and moved quickly to the warm firelight that even now was pushing back the clinging shadows. He wrapped his fingers around her upper arms a little tighter then he intended and shook her gently.

"Why didn't you answer me Sasha?" he demanded.

"Sorry....I was making sure the flu was open," she replied giving him a look that clearly indicated he was a little unhinged.

Quin released her upper arms and took a deep breath, "I'm sorry Sash ... I ... I just..."

"Don't worry about it, now that we have a fire though we should probably bring our stuff in here and try to get some rest. There's an old couch and a couple of chairs over there and somebody could always sleep on the desktop," Sasha waved off his concern just like she had done so many times before.

Quin's jaw worked hard but he nodded at the soundness of the idea. They could always use some of the water in their canteens and mix up a meal over the fire. They hadn't eaten since earlier in the day and now that they had a fire Quin realized just how hungry and tired he really was.

"Tristan, why don't we go grab the bags and make sure the doors are still secure?"

Tristan nodded and followed Quin back to the door where Morgan still hesitated just inside the threshold.

"Everything okay?" Morgan asked casting a glance towards Sasha's back as she bent to stoke the guttering flames.

"Yeah, everything is fine," Quin replied and pushed past him.

Back in the main part of the library the air didn't feel as thick and oppressive as it had in the office and, if at all possible, the inky darkness wasn't as stygian black either. Quin breathed deeply and frowned to himself. His little voice of reason was telling him that they should not be in the office, they should stay in the front of the library where escape would be easiest if need be. The office was a dead end, if they were trapped there then there was nothing but death waiting for them. He shook his head to rid himself of such morbid thoughts. This was going to be a long night.

"I don't think we should go back in there," Tristan whispered, echoing Quin's own thoughts.

"I know but we can't leave Sasha back there alone," Quin replied as he grabbed his pack and hefted Sasha's onto his forearm.

"You aren't serious about us hanging out back there are you?" Morgan asked following suit.

"I think right now we should just go back and try to heat up some food since there is a fire. Then we can discuss where we want to spend the rest of the night. I still think we need to sleep in shifts."

"Fine, I volunteer for the first shift," Morgan replied.

Quin could read clearly in Morgan's expression his own feelings that he didn't want to be trapped in the back of the library. Quin nodded and led the way to the back. When they entered the office a cheery fire was blazing brightly fending off the gloomy shadows and chill. Maybe they were just overreacting. Quin would reserve his opinion until after they had eaten.

Sasha smiled brightly and motioned to an area around the fireplace. She had already pulled the chairs closer and shoved the couch in to a position facing the flickering flames. It looked almost homey.

"See we have warmth and somewhere to rest. We can make something to eat and try to get some sleep to pass this awful night. By sun up we can get on our way and leave this place behind us, just another story for the trail," she said sounding as if she were trying to convince all of them that nothing was off about the whole situation.

Quin nodded as a melancholy slipped over him.

Let her make believe everything is going to be fine, he told himself, *time enough for tears and regret later.*

They all settled on the worn musty furniture and pulled out a few packs of dehydrated food to mix with a portion of water from their canteens. In no time the small cooking pot released the aroma of beef stew and Morgan's stomach rumbled loudly.

"I didn't realize just how hungry I was," he laughed as he patted his protesting belly and gladly took the cup of soup Sasha handed him.

They all chuckled and dug into the soup. The mood had lightened considerably and if it weren't for the niggling fact that they were stuck in a building they would have almost felt comfortable just like they had so many other evenings around the campfire. Tristan told them about the time he and his uncle had been fishing off of the small barrier island he had grown up on when they were caught up in a storm. The wind had come up from nowhere and then the storm had rolled in. It had all been a part of island life for him so they weathered through it.

After giving the cups and small cook pot a quick clean up, Sasha stored them away in the back packs. She was almost domesticated, Quin reflected as he watched her flit about the room unfurling sleeping bags and situating their packs. It was a side he had never really thought she possessed. Maybe he was just cynical. The thought tugged down the corners of his mouth. Maybe he wasn't cynical after all. What did he really know about Sasha? It wasn't like they had all been together very long. For that matter what did he really know about any of them?

He cast his gaze about the room glancing from first one smiling face to another. He didn't really know these people after all. Sure they had built a camaraderie on their trek north along the trail but still, did he really know them? Did he know what demons may lurk in their minds? What darkness dwelled in their souls? The questions whispered through his mind as if uttered by the low soft voice of someone else. Quin rubbed his face and tried to shake off the sudden urge to shout the questions at them. What was he thinking? Why was he even thinking such things? He caught Tristan's smiling gaze and returned the gesture. This was Tristan, the soon to be marine biologist and Morgan who didn't give a flying fig about anything but the immediate present.

His gaze fell on the final member of their party and glided across her flaxen braids. Unconsciously he licked his lips then looked away before anyone could see the unfulfilled longing in his eyes. She was captivating. She was beautiful. She was stubborn and she was obstinate. She was everything he was looking for in a woman but couldn't have. She was a trust fund baby and he; he was just a poor kid that had decided to hike the trail to find himself. There was no way she would ever give him the time of day. The thought brought back his grumpy melancholy and sent him to his feet.

Everyone jumped at the sudden movement and Quin cursed himself as a fool.

"Sorry," he mumbled, "I'll take first watch. You guys try to get some sleep."

Before anyone could argue, Quin turned and strode forcefully from the room. He preferred the quiet solace of the darkened library to the cheerful firelight of the office. At least in the darkness no one could see his anger. Quin wandered back through the stacks of moldering books to the circulation desk and tested the piece of furniture. It may have sat there for years weathered by neglect but it was still sturdy. He climbed atop the desk and sat cross legged resting his elbows on his knees. He silently reviled himself of every manner of idiot that he was. He knew better than to wish for things he couldn't have.

Time slipped by in a slow march towards midnight as the heat of the afternoon became nothing more than a memory inside the tomb of the old school house. The heat of Quin's self-recriminations died away and he found himself shivering slightly against the chill of the dank library. He didn't know how long he had sat in one spot but the muscles in his back protested when he moved to jump down from the table. His legs screamed and threatened to spasm uncontrollably. Slowly he stretched first one, then the other, working the kinks out of his calf muscles. He really should be paying more attention instead of thinking about her.

As if on cue, Quin caught a glimpse of her shining golden hair as she made her way through the stacks towards him. She carried with her a small light that cast a soft warm glow across the rows of books and sea of tables. Her serene face was pale in the darkness but her eyes were warm and bright as they stayed steady on him. Quin's mouth was suddenly dry and he wasn't sure what he should say. He opened his mouth but she touched a finger to her lips in a gesture for him to keep silent. Quin nodded and stood still beside the circulation desk he had climbed off of.

She came closer and he could just make out the hint of her perfume. Something very expensive and ultra-feminine. His mouth was suddenly flooded with saliva and he had to swallow several times to clear it.

He rubbed a clammy palm across his jeans and felt his stomach knot in anticipation. What was he thinking would happen? She was just coming to take his place as lookout that was all. He repeated the thought to himself as she glided across the last of the space between them and set the small light down on the desk. Odd but he didn't remember that light in any of their packs before.

She placed her finger under his chin and urged his gaze from its inspection of the light back to her. She dropped her gaze coyly and then looked up at him through her lashes.

"Di...." he began but she pressed her fingertip to his lips silencing the question he was about to ask.

His lips pursed into a pucker on their own accord and pressed a light kiss against her finger.

I shouldn't have done that, he thought and would have said so if she hadn't moved in closer to him. The smell of perfume swelled and enveloped his senses as she pressed her soft breasts against his chest. He stifled a groan and cursed himself for a fool again as he stepped away from her. Sasha didn't take the hint; she moved forward again and pressed her breasts against his chest once more.

"Is there something wrong? Tristan and Morgan are asleep, we're completely alone. No one will know," she whispered as she nibbled at his jaw.

Quin groaned as she slid her questing fingers into the soft hair at the nape of his neck and pulled his head down for a deep kiss. Quin's eyes slid shut as he gave in and savored the taste of her lips pressed to his. She was intoxicating. Her scent grew and enveloped the immediate area as he wrapped his arms around her tiny waist and pulled her tightly against him. What could it hurt to give in to this temptation? She was clearly willing and wanted him as much as he wanted her. An electric current flitted through him as he parted her lips and slipped the tip of his tongue inside. Somewhere in the back of his brain an alarm was going off telling him that this was not right. The sensualist in him ignored the alarm and continued to partake of what she was offering.

A low howl from far below the library windows cut through the lethargy that was creeping in to his bones. Another alarm rattled through his brain as he tried to remember why they were in the building. The warmth of Sasha's embrace tried to pull him back in to the realm of earthly delights as her fingers tightened almost painfully in his hair. Her mouth grew more demanding as they crushed his lips against his teeth. A feral growl rumbled through her throat as the overwhelming scent of her perfume threatened to choke him.

Quin fought against her steely grip and felt part of his hair yank free of his scalp as she continued to fight him for contact. He howled in pain and struck her before he could stop himself. She faltered a step but was back on him in seconds, grasping and clawing at his chest and face. The light wavered but in the fraction of time before it went out he could see that Sasha's once beautiful face was now a mass of flaking rotting skin that dripped from her partially exposed skull.

"What's the matter Quin? Don't you find me attractive anymore?" she hissed as she continued to try to make contact with his mouth again.

"Get away you demon bitch!" he shouted as he shoved at her clinging body.

"Quin, what's going on?" Morgan asked as he shuffled out into the vast library to take his place at watch.

Quin jerked around to look at Morgan's pale visage as he approached through the stacks. He turned to look at Sasha but found himself standing alone in the middle of the room near the circulation desk. What the hell had just happened? Had any of it been real? Morgan stopped beside him and stared at the same spot of thin air.

"Are you okay Quin? You look like you just saw a ghost," Morgan replied as he tossed his pack on the expanse of the circulation desk and then hopped up on it, settling into the spot Quin had just vacated.

"I thought I just saw Sasha," Quin mumbled, afraid to give breath to the horror he had just witnessed.

"Sasha's in back sleeping like a baby. You need to go on back there and get some shut eye. I'll take over," Morgan yawned and wiped away the last vestiges of sleep from his eyes.

Should Quin tell Morgan what he thought he had seen? Would Morgan think he was insane? Quin had a sinking feeling that he would so he opted to keep silent. It had to be the building and the stress of the situation getting to him. Maybe it was the mold, after all some mold was toxic and could kill a human being. Maybe it was causing him to hallucinate as well? Quin shook the thought off and sighed heavily. He really didn't want to spend any more time in the librarian's office but his pack and sleeping bag were back there.

"Just keep your eyes peeled Morgan, I think there is something strange going on with this building but I can't put my finger on it," Quin mumbled as he ran a weary hand through his hair and winced at the soreness in the back of his scalp.

His fingers played across the bald patch of flesh as the memory of Sasha jerking out some of his hair flitted back through his mind. Had it actually happened?

"Morgan I think....." Quin trailed off when he found himself standing alone in the circulation desk area.

Where had Morgan disappeared to? What the hell was going on? Quin pinched himself and gave an involuntary yelp of pain as his arm throbbed. He was definitely awake. He turned a full circle, examining the room for any indication that this wasn't a nightmare. He stopped abruptly and started at the exit sign above the library doors. It glowed a soft red in the blackness of the room. Had the sign been on before and he hadn't noticed it? If so then the building had to have power? How could they have missed that?

He opened his mouth to call to them to try the light switches when the faint sound of shuffling left the unspoken words dying on his lips. He stepped closer to the door to listen. A faint drag and thump sounded on the other side as if from a distance. It continued in an unrelenting pace down the hallway. It paused once and in his mind's eye he estimated that it was at the T junction in the hallway as if trying to decide whether to come towards the library or go do the other side of the hallway towards the other classrooms. He willed it to continue to the other classrooms.

After what seemed like an eternity the drag and slid footstep resumed its unerring course towards the library doors. Damn! What should he do? Quin stepped back and looked for a weapon, anything he could use to swat whatever was on the other side of the door. He found a large year book and hefted it as if it were a baseball bat. The drag slide step stopped on the other side of the door.

Silence reigned like a bloody queen as he held his breath listening for whatever sound would come next. The metal bar door handles rattled violently as the unknown being on the other side of the door tried to get in. Quin's heart lodged in his throat as his muscles contracted painfully. He was coiled and ready to spring into action when the wild jiggling of the handles stopped as abruptly as they had started. Against his own best judgment he crept closer to the door and pressed an ear against it.

"Quin, Quin it's me, Tristan, open the door man. Let me in," Tristan's voice croaked in a hushed tone from the other side of the wooden barricade.

"Shut up, I don't know who you are but my friend Tristan is in here, not out there," Quin replied as he stepped back from the door.

"Quin let me in dammit! There's something wrong with this place, there's something wrong with Sasha. She got Morgan...did you hear me? Morgan's dead and Sasha killed him. Let me in Quin!" Tristan was fairly shouting from the other side of the door as he began to beat wildly against it.

"Shut up!" Quin yelled, "Tristan and Morgan are in here with me. You're not real! You're not real! You're not real!"

A low throaty chuckle rolled through the door, "Are you so sure about that?"

Quin stepped away from the door as the handle began to jiggle violently again. He wished his had a gun instead of a damn yearbook. At least with a gun he could blast the hell out of whatever was on the other side of the door. The high pitched cackle grated along his nerve endings again as the thought left his brain.

"You can't kill what you can't see," the voice taunted from the other side of the door.

The hell I can't, Quin thought.

His eyes roamed around the room again searching for anything he could use against the being on the other side of the door. The faint smell of fresh paint wafted on the fresh breeze that whistled through the cracked window pane. Quin watched as the crack in the window slowly disappeared and the pane was once again complete. The fresh smell of disinfectant hung heavily in the air as the scent of mold vanished.

"Morgan, Tristan!" Quin shouted as the electric hum of the fluorescent lights overhead winked on.

The light was blinding after so much darkness and Quin blinked rapidly trying to adjust to the onslaught on his dilated pupils. The maniacal laughter from the other side of the door cut through his brain as he dropped the yearbook on the floor and fumbled towards the back of the room. He bumped into desks and cursed as his shins throbbed. His eyes adjusted and he sprinted through the stacks to the librarian's office. He flipped the lights on and gagged at the sight before him.

Tristan and Morgan's mummified corpses lay swaddled in their sleeping bags, their sunken eyes staring blankly at the ceiling. Their slack jaws were open in silent screams as the terror that had seized them was frozen on their features for all eternity. The brown leathery skin clung to their skeletal remains as if every ounce of life had been sucked from them.

Quin gave them a wide birth, trying to avoid the accusation in the dead men's eyes as he grabbed for his pack. He threw his sleeping bag across their faces and hastily whispered a prayer for forgiveness as he jerked the lighter from Morgan's pack and searched for the tinder they used when starting the camp fire. If this was how it was going to end he was going to go out on his own terms.

He grabbed the brass lamp from the desktop and broke off the old green shade. Tearing the flannel shirt into strips he wrapped them tightly around the swing arm of the lamp.

"I'm sorry guys," he whispered then set the tinder on fire on top of the sleeping bags where Tristan and Morgan's corpses lay.

He donned his pack and strode back out into the library carrying his makeshift torch. *Better to die outside with those demon dogs then be eaten alive by the damn building*, he thought. He paused near the library door and flicked the lighter. The flint sputtered then finally shot forth a tiny flame. He paused in lighting the flannel when he looked down at the picture staring up at him from the open pages of the yearbook. Bright shining blue eyes stared out of a face that looked to be seventeen years old. Long golden braids cascaded across her shoulders. The caption below the picture read:

In remembrance of Sasha Beaudraux gone but not forgotten.

Quin's hand shook as he stared at the same blue eyes that had smiled into his not so long ago. Her smiling face was now taunting him from the yearbook. He kicked the book violently across the floor and set the flame to the flannel shirt and shoved the bookcases out of the way. Jerking the door open he came face to face with the bright white hallway and the curious faces that peered at him from the classroom doors.

"Stay back or I will burn it down I swear!" he shouted as he sprinted down the hall to the staircase.

An unearthly scream rattled through the building as he ran down the staircase to the open foyer below.

"There is no running in the halls," Sasha's voice called from the staircase.

Quin paused at the door and turned to see her standing at top of the stairs flanked on all sides by children. She smiled broadly and pointed at him. They descended the stairs like a wave of faceless creatures with claw like hands outstretched grasping for him. They tore at his clothes and hair and clawed at his face and eyes. Quin waved the torch lighting first one then another on fire as he felt for the front door handle behind him.

He managed to jerk the door open as Sasha shrieked and raced towards him. The children reeled about knocking into the doors and desks setting the building and its contents on fire.

"You can't do this!" Sasha screamed as she wrapped her hands around his neck choking the life from him.

Quin grabbed her wrists and squeezed feeling the bones crack beneath his grip. He fell out the door taking Sasha with him. The shriek grew in intensity as all of the windows in the school exploded in a shower of glass. Quin landed on his back, coughing as the first rays of sunlight burst over the mountain tops. He laid there, the smell of smoke still strong in his nostrils, staring up at the old hulk of the run down school.

"Son, what the hell are you doing out here?" a croaky voice asked from somewhere beyond his range of vision.

Quin rolled over onto his side and stared at an elderly man in bib overalls and a faded red baseball cap.

"I got lost and had to stay in here last night," Quin coughed.

"Are you crazy son? Nobody goes in there and lives," the farmer replied, "Come on I'll give you a ride in to town."

"My friends...." Quin began.

"If they were in there with you I daresay they ain't coming out," the farmer replied.

Quin faltered as he stood shakily. He nodded sadly and grabbed his pack from the steps where it had fallen when he tumbled out the door.

"What is this place?" he asked as he followed the farmer back to the beat up truck that idled not far from where he had lain.

"Resurrection school house, been abandoned for years," the farmer replied as he climbed in the cab.

"Why?" Quin couldn't help but ask.

"A young girl name Sasha Beaudraux died there a while back. She was helping put away books in the library when she fell off one of the ladders and broke her neck. It wasn't long after that the building caught on fire, burnt everyone up. It was a tragedy," the farmer replied.

Quin swallowed hard and glanced out the rear window at the retreating hulk of the building. He could just make out Sasha as she stood in the doorway flanked on either side by Tristan and Morgan.

ABOUT THE AUTHOR

M.D. Martin was born and raised in Abingdon, VA. She first began writing the Legends of William's Point series in 1995 while attending Virginia Highlands Community College. She has been published in the Bristol Herald Courier Newspaper, The Sage Literary Magazine, and Treasured poems of America. One of her Christmas stories has also appeared on the WABN radio station. When she isn't writing she is an avid reader and loves the Pendergast novels by Douglas Preston and Lincoln Child, Edgar Allen Poe, and Janet Evanovich's Stephanie Plum series. She also enjoys photography, camping, cooking, and spending time with family and friends.

www.ingramcontent.com/pod-product-compliance
Lightning Source LLC
Chambersburg PA
CBHW052009170626
46808CB00007B/2841